Www.LarryRedmond.Com

Also by Larry Redmond

A Feast of Peonies (2003)

The Last and Final King (2003)

Satan's Anvil and other stories (2004)

A Lake of Fire (1972, 2006)

The Reward of the Fool (2009)

Why to Kill a Billionaire (2015)

Self-Absorbed II:
Nude Self-Portraits and Still Lifes (2017)

Death to the Equestrians

Death
to the
Equestrians
by
Larry Redmond

Penknife Press   Chicago, Illinois

Copyright © 2017 by Larry Redmond
All rights reserved under International and Pan-American Copyright Conventions.
Published in the United States of America by Penknife Press, Ltd., Chicago, Illinois.

ISBN 978-1-59997-034-9

Library of Congress Control Number: 2017942279

Manufactured in the United States of America

For the great day of his wrath is come; and who shall be able to stand?

The Holy Bible
Revelations 6:17

"Man, what be wrong with white folks?"

"I swear to God I don't know," I answered.

"But it's got to be something wrong with them motherfuckers."

"I know, I know."

I had not seen Reverend Milton in years, literally. He was a hulking man, six-six, two hundred and fifty pounds. He wasn't fat, and he wasn't muscular. To my knowledge, he never worked out. He was mocha-colored and clean-shaven with short, curly hair, the kind we used to call good hair. Maybe whoever he got that hair from was the same somebody after whom he managed to be so heavy without being fat. I guess it was just in his genes, divine providence, and my having run into him now can only be described as the same kind of divine providence.

I had been on my way to the bank. The bank was on the corner of Lawrence and Broadway. It was warm out. Spring was in the air. I could smell food being cooked at one of the local restaurants. The scent was heavy with curry and olive oil. A young white boy zipped along in the bike lane on a red,

Larry Redmond

white and blue skateboard, his long, yellow hair tipped with green flapping in the breeze.

Normally, I never went to the bank. Since getting home from our last op back in the middle of winter, I stayed close to home a lot. Maybe I was getting too old for this shit. Maybe I was getting soft. Maybe I was getting scared. And since it was already six in the evening, the bank was probably already closed anyway. But I thought I'd check, just in case it was not. I think I needed to order some deposit forms or something. I didn't even remember for sure. But there I was, walking south on Broadway just north of Lawrence. I was on the east side of the street.

All of a sudden, I could hear the chords of Senior Blues being played on the piano. The music was coming from the Green Mill across the street. Someone had opened the door to leave, and the chords escaped unnoticed by everyone except me. Just hearing them sent a rush of images and memories flashing through my mind, images of being stationed in the Air Force in Darmstadt, Germany, back in the day.

I had been young back then, fresh from the States, new to overseas travel. There was a joint back then that all the brothers in the military stationed in that immediate area would go to out in Griesheim called the Fetzenkeller. The place was a dive. Naked hardwood floors that hadn't been polished maybe ever. Rough-hewn tables with thick legs and hardback benches and chairs.

The patrons were rough-hewn as well. Women with thick makeup and heavy lipstick. Servicemen with heavy pockets and thick dicks looking to put all of it into one of those gussied up women. The bar had huge, two-gallon jars of hard boiled eggs and pickles set off to one side. I don't know who ate them. Certainly, we never did. We always ordered schnitzel and rice to cut the effects of all the cognac and gin and Schwarzer Kater we drank. That was where the battle of Griesheim was fought.

The battle of Griesheim started one night after everybody in the place had been drinking way too much gin. Some air force dude referred to an army soldier as a low-IQ-beetle-crusher. As a matter of routine, air force personnel referred to army personnel as ground pounders because they marched a lot, like we did in basic training at Lackland. The underlying implication was that they were not too bright. Who, after all, would pound the ground? Never mind that we did when we all first joined. We were a bunch of snooty bastards, but the soldiers tolerated us good-heartedly. They knew we meant the term with some degree of humility, because they knew that we knew that many of them were smart, and had merely been drafted.

Being called a low-IQ-beetle-crusher, however, was a direct insult. Naturally, the ground pounder took umbrage. He was short and wide across the back and shoulders. The airman was tall and skinny and pale. After the insult, the soldier took a swing and knocked the air force dude out cold. He almost had to jump the reach the airman's jaw, but reach it he did. Before *Mutter*-- that's what we all called the fat, little white-haired proprietor-- could yell, "closing time," all hell broke loose. The air force got its ass kicked that night, and the army retained bragging rights to being the baddest outfit in Darmstadt.

The Fetzenkeller was a dive, but it had Senior Blues by Horace Silver on the jukebox. That might have been its only saving grace, and hearing it now caused an irresistible urge to rise up in me. I dashed across the street, almost oblivious of the traffic. A royal blue Camero with wishbone wheels blared its horn as I forced it to veer into the other lane to avoid slowing down for me.

I paid the cover to a young man in denim jeans and a Cubs T-shirt, and made my way straight over to the piano. As I approached, I thought I recognized the man hunched over the keys. The problem was that I didn't know this particular person even played piano. There were several other patrons near the piano, an elderly man crushing an aluminum beer can with one hand, a young woman with a wide smile and squeaky voice pretending to be dazzled by his show of strength. I had to get closer to be sure. The closer I got, the more sure I became. The man was big. The "M" his hairline formed over his high and broad forehead was the clincher. It was Reverend Milton. His fingers were so big, I wondered how he managed to hit only one key at a time. But somehow, he did. With each movement, he angled his hands just right to strike only the keys he intended to strike. Watching him play was like watching the tutu-clad hippopotamus in Fantasia dance. It was incongruous, but it worked.

He looked up at me, and resumed a conversation we had had years earlier while getting high near Montrose Harbor. He resumed as if no time at all had elapsed.

"They don't know shit," he continued, "but they think they know everything."

"I know," I said again, "I know."

He was animated in his disgust. I had heard this diatribe from him before, more than once. It was like a script that we improvised on whenever the topic of white people arose. We jammed on it like trumpet and saxophone players jamming on a standard melody.

The last time was when we were over by Montrose Harbor getting high off reefer. It was warm that evening. Seagulls rode the evening breeze, and I was fixated on the bobbing of boats rocking on the waves, their masts swaying back and forth. There was a wounded seagull hiding in the bushes just off the water's edge. One of its wings was damaged, the left one. That wing drooped almost to the ground, and it was as if the bird was waiting for something to come along and kill it. It knew it couldn't escape whatever fate awaited it.

That might have been the last time I got high. I could still remember the way the earth felt like it had begun spinning in the opposite direction and the boats out in the harbor bobbing and swaying contributing to my discomfort.

Milton had been going on and on about Nietzsche and the racist he was. Milton had toked the joint, and inhaled the smoke with a loud hiss, his dark lips poked out like he was kissing somebody. He tried to talk and hold the smoke in at the same time. Unsuccessful, he would exhale sharply, and sniff. Racism was his message then, and it was his message now.

"They think killing a nigger is a rite of passage. You ain't a real honky 'til you kill a nigger." He leaned into the piano phrase he was playing, and gave an Errol Garner-like groan, "Umh."

"Yeah," I said. "And they're killing children from behind the safety of a badge."

"Some rite," Milton said. "They need to stop being so scared." Then he dismissed our conversation in favor of allowing himself to sink deeper into his music, his bratwurst fingers carefully selecting which keys to punch.

He sank into the music; I sank into thought fueled by the chords he was playing. It's a funny thing about societal fear, the fear that white cops feel when confronting Black people.

Mo'Dear told me once that there was someplace a

Black woman could go that a Black man could *not* go. She was big by then, having gained a hundred pounds after Daddy died. She waved her chubby index finger in my face as she spoke. "That's just a fact of life in America," she had said. I supposed this was her way of preparing me for the real world, a world where Black women had privileges Black men did not.

Years later, Grandma Daughter told me the same thing. I was sure their comments were not coordinated. I didn't know where that someplace was, but I began to believe it. I began to believe there was some mystical place where Black women could get to that was somehow restricted from Black men. Many years after that, I realized that someplace was where white men allowed them to go that they wouldn't allow Black men to go. It was many, many years after that when I realized why. White men were fucking Black women, and allowing them to be with them in their bastions of power, bastions where even white women were not allowed. And from time to time, they might even take a Black woman's suggestion, and make a decision based on it. Pussy and the prospect of getting it again and again has that effect on men.

Mo'Dear and Grandma Daughter knew who I was even when I did not, and wanted to make sure I understood the rules of the game, rules created by white men for white men and the beneficiaries of their generosity. Once I understood what they meant, I resented it.

Milton finished his rendition of Senior Blues, and began idly plunking the keys, as if searching for another tune to present itself. "They need to see a shrink," he said, "all of 'em."

He played a few bars of Misty, then abandoned it.

"They need to see Bobby Wright."

"Bobby who?" I asked.

"Dr. Bobby Wright. *The* Dr. Bobby Wright."

"Who the fuck is *the* Dr. Bobby Wright?"

Milton toyed with Love for Sale, then abandoned that, too.

I couldn't take my eyes off his hands as he played. I kept looking for the magic that allowed adjacent keys to be missed as he plucked key after key after key, sometimes multiple keys at once.

"Bobby was a bad motherfuckin' psychologist. He's the one who diagnosed white people as having a psychopathic racial personality disorder."

"Aw, okay," I said.

9   Larry Redmond

"He's the one who named the ailment Tecumseh recognized back in 1811."

Milton was like a walking encyclopedia. He was always coming up with obscure facts about shit nobody else ever even heard of.

"Who the fuck is Tecumseh?" I asked.

"Tecumseh was a Shawnee chief back in the day. It was he who said that the white race was a wicked race. The hunting grounds were fast disappearing and they were driving the red man farther and farther west. Let the white race parish whence they came.'"

"*Who* said that?" I asked. I guess I was hoping he would utter a name that I easily recognized. He didn't.

Before today, it had been years since I had seen Milton. Thinking back, I hadn't seen him since after he needed space from me in order to feel safe. I could not even remember what he needed to feel safe from.

He began the first few bars of 'Round Midnight, then began to settle into it. He gave another Errol Garner-like grunt, and I knew our conversation was over. As I left the lounge, I still had the music rattling around in my head. I never did figure out how he missed hitting the wrong keys. The elderly man who was crushing beer cans with one hand left just before me. He was with the young woman with the wide smile who was pretending to be dazzled. Maybe she wasn't pretending.

"You were so strong in there," she squeaked. Her toothy smile was radiant.

"Yeah, I know," he said, and slipped his arm around her waist as they headed south along Broadway. He pinched her on the ass, and she giggled.

By now, it was almost dark. The smells of curry and olive oil were replaced by the smell of diesel fumes from passing buses and trucks with red and blue signage for moving services and storage. The remembrances of my conversations with Milton had me in a funk. It seemed at odds. The music was uplifting. But the conversation that went with the music was depressing. That's when the answer to Milton's what-be-wrong-with-white-folks question came to me. They were consumed with fear, a deep fear down in their bones. What they feared was Black men. And with good reason. We some dangerous motherfuckers! They knew better than we who we truly were. And they quaked in that knowledge. More importantly, they knew the evil they had done, and they knew that eventually they were going to have to pay for it.

I felt a sense of satisfaction at having reached that conclusion.

Then, in a moment akin to an epiphany, I realized that these motherfuckers were afraid of *me*. I stopped in my tracks, and almost as if on cue, I heard a car screeching to a halt at the corner of Broadway and Granville. I was on my way back to my apartment, and the notion struck me like a wing chun punch to the sternum. They were not afraid of me in particular, because they didn't know me in particular. They were afraid of everybody *like* me.

I began to wonder how they knew how dangerous we really were. Had they been studying us? I resumed my trek back home pass the post office, past auto repair shops with yellow signs for oil changes and muffler repairs, past the super market with huge plate glass windows, and past martial arts dojos with silhouettes of high kicking boxers stenciled on the doors. They had been studying us for years. They had seen us naked in the hot Alabama sun picking cotton, and they wondered how we did it. They had seen us fight one another, sometimes to the death. They had seen us fuck one another, sometimes for hours. They *knew* what we could do. They had studied us way longer than we had studied them. And we had rarely if ever stopped and studied ourselves. The reason was simple. We took what we do for granted.

I remembered when I first saw the power that I had. Like now, I was walking home from meeting with a friend. Only then, I was about thirteen. It was a route I had never taken before, pass red brick apartment buildings that looked like castles with mown green lawns. As I walked their way, sparrows leaped into flight like little super heros racing off to save who-knows-what?

Back then, Mo'Dear, Grandma Daughter and I didn't live in an apartment building. We lived on the first floor of a two-story building on the 1400 block of Saint Louis Avenue. We moved to the west side in order to put more distance between us and where Daddy died. The landlord lived on the second floor with his wife and three routy children. At the time, I had often wondered who lived in these castles, and what life in them must have been like.

As I walked, I could see two boys standing in front of one of the buildings to the left along my path.

They wore blond crew cuts and white T-shirts with the sleeves rolled up exposing their muscular arms all the way up to the shoulder. One of them nodded to the other. I knew I did not recognize them, so I continued on. As I approached, one of them, the bigger one of the two, the one with the rumpled tan pants and bright red bleeding heart tattoo on his right forearm, called out to me.

"Hey, you," he said. "Come 'ere?"

I kept walking, still in my revery. Seeing me walk pass, he grabbed my arm to stop me.

"Didn't you hear me say, come 'ere?" he said.

"Huh?" I was confused. I didn't fully understand his question or what it's real relevance was.

He smacked me. He was a full head taller than I was. He had a wide head and pointed chin and crooked teeth. One of his upper front teeth had grown in twisted, perpendicular to the others. With his open hand, he smacked me upside the left side of my head. The skin on the palm of his hand felt rough and raspy on my face. My ears rang with music that sounded like a choir warming up. My eyes watered, and my nose began to run. There was a salty taste in my mouth. I wondered if my teeth were bleeding. I realized somehow that I was tasting my tears. He smacked me again, and my knees began to buckle. I could feel myself sinking to the ground.

That's when it happened. All of a sudden, I was strong. I could feel a creature-like character rising up in me. I put one hand on the sidewalk to balance myself, then I stood up. My attacker kept hitting me, but I couldn't feel it. He was pounding me with his fist on my head and shoulders to keep me from standing up, but I was too powerful for him. He tried to wrestle me, but my feet were like granite on the sidewalk. He couldn't move me. I reached up and clutched his throat with my left hand and squeezed as hard as I could. He grabbed my wrist with both his hands trying to break my grip. Both his hands had that rough skin, and his fingernails were edged with gunk. He tried to yank away, but nothing worked for him. I felt invincible. I was the creature, and the creature *was* invincible.

I was aware of everything around me, the texture of the sidewalk through the soles of my shoes, the moisture in and the movement of the air, the sweat gathering on his skin and the bones in his throat. I was acutely aware that he did not smell like Black boys, and I marveled at the fact. I could see the

15   Larry Redmond

other boy, his friend, step back in fear, his steely blue eyes widened. This boy was smaller than both my attacker and me. He wore the same tan pants and white T-shirt as my attacker, but his sleeves were not rolled up as high. His mouth was agape at seeing his much larger friend being pushed back so easily.

I decided to push my attacker in the direction of the building. I didn't know where that decision came from, but I knew it was the right thing to do. I angled him towards my left approaching the building entrance. He resisted, but to no avail. My grip on his throat was too firm. I marched him along the walkway. He was forced to peddle backwards on dangly legs as I strode forward. His friend kept pace with us hoping, I supposed, to see his buddy rebound and rally.

Within seconds, I had my attacker pinned against the brick facade, my left hand still clutching his throat. I leaned into my grip. His breathing was strained. He was beginning to pant. I drew my right fist back to pound it into his face. He knew what was coming. I could feel him start to panic. His body began to tremble. He released his hold on my left wrist with one of his hands in order to block the strike about to be delivered with my right hand. His free hand gripped my right fist to keep me from drawing it back.

Ironically, at the exact moment that he gripped my fist, I began to wonder what was going to happen to my fist as I pushed it through his face, and hit the brick wall behind his head. So I paused drawing my fist back until I answered that question in my head. That's when I realized that I could simply push my fist right through the wall as well. I resumed drawing my fist back. There was nothing he could do to stop this. He began to panic again. His whole body quaked. He released his other hand from my left wrist allowing me to squeeze his throat unchallenged, and committed both his hands to stopping me from pulling my right fist back in order to crush his face to a pulp. It wasn't enough. I easily broke his hold.

That was what *I* and *we* could do. *That* was why *we* were dangerous to them. And *that* was why they were afraid of us.

Walking home now, I turned east towards Sheridan Road. There was a strong smell of sewage in the air. In a way, I felt sorry for them. Try as they might, there was *nothing* they could do to stop us. I knew that deep inside, they knew that as well, but were in denial. But then, how does a race of people come to grips with the knowledge of their own extinction? Unlike Native Americans who had their land stolen, or Africans who had their freedom stolen, whites were having their existence taken from them. That was a hard pill to swallow.

I flexed my hands trying to remember the feeling in them the day those boys stopped me. It was gone. All I could feel now was the tightness from all the Iron Palm training I had done over the years. I became aware of the light shining from the long string of cobra-style streetlights along my way, and I picked up my pace.

Once back at home, I turned on the TV to see if there was any coverage of the job the crew and I had pulled. There wasn't. Just some blonde woman wearing too red lipstick going on and on about how entitlement programs were ruining the economy. The job was long enough ago that it was old news now anyway. Eventually, the news turned to sports, and showed clips of some guy leaping against the outfield wall to shag a fly ball, his crimson red cap sailing off in the process.

Even without the news, I could still feel the rush

of victory! The taste was still sweet! We eliminated our target, the Cach twins, the entire board of directors of their pharmaceutical manufacturing company, and over half of the major shareholders.

Arrogant bastards! They thought the guards at their annual retreat could protect them! But we were ready. We reconnoitered, we planned, we practiced, we drilled. In the end, they were no match.

Still high on our success, I ordered Chinese, shrimp egg foo yung, and spent the evening watching Perry Mason reruns. Perry Mason never lost a case.

That night, I had a dream about Mo'Dear. I had not dreamed about her in years, but tonight, here she was. The dream wasn't long or involved. But its impact on me was profound. I was driving a vehicle of some kind in a park. The vehicle was small and fully enclosed. It moved slowly. The people in the park reacted as if this kind of vehicle were a normal thing to see. So in the dream, everything seemed normal. Then Mo'Dear walked across the path of the vehicle from right to left. She looked in the windshield at me, then looked away. She didn't recognize me. That's when I noticed that her

Larry Redmond

hairstyle was from 60 or more years ago. It was a pageboy, curled under below the nape of her neck. And she was still thin and cute. Somehow, I was riding in the past, in a time before my daddy died. After Daddy died, Mo'Dear picked up a hundred pounds in weight. In my dream, she mentioned to someone within my hearing that she was looking for her son. I knew that meant she was looking for me. But she had just seen me, and didn't react. Therefore, she was looking for me as a child.

As I drove by her location, leaves began falling from the trees and obscuring my view. It wasn't autumn, so the leaves were still green, and they swirled around my vehicle as if I were on the inside of a tornado. A part of me began to wonder how it happened that green leaves were suddenly falling from the trees. But as quickly as I had begun to wonder, the leaves stopped swirling, and I stopped wondering. I craned my neck to the left to see if I could see the child that was me. I couldn't. I began to wonder if I could find me as a child. Then, in the dream, I got scared. I didn't know what would happen if I found me as a child. Would I cease to exist? Would the time-space continuum be permanently disrupted? I started remembering old episodes of Star Trek and movies like Back to the Future and Timecop looking for clues as to what the rules of time travel were. The notion that I might cease to exist so upset me that I woke up. It took some hours to get back to sleep again, and by then my rest was uneasy. I couldn't help wondering what would have happened had I found the young boy that was me.

II

Being God does not make you invincible. Jesus knew that. He knew that He had to die. That's why He wept. I knew that I, too, was God, and I also knew that I could and would die one day. At least this body that I ride around in. That's the thing about getting old. It sucks. Granted, it beats the alternative by a wide margin, but it still sucks, even when you've experienced the alternative and risen from it. It sucks.

Part of the reason it sucks is that it is a disappointment. When you're young, you think there are things that you will know when you get old. Important things. You think at some level that you will have figured out the meaning of life. And at one level, you do. But that's not the level that we function at day to day. At the day-to-day level, it simply was not true. Old folks were merely children in worn out bodies. And we didn't know shit! Not at the day-to-day level. We were still as amazed by life as when we were young, running and skipping and jumping. Inside, nothing's changed. The change was only on the outside.

But, sometimes there *were* things that you learned, things that you learned on the inside. On the non-day-to-day level, I had learned who the Beasts were, the families who ride humanity like horses, horses whose colors were white and red and black and pale yellow. I had learned that the horses will throw off their riders one day, and trample them under their hooves like blades of dried grasses.

The red horse, the great russet stallion of the west, will trample the warmongers invading the Democratic Republic of Congo, the Central African Republic, Afghanistan, Iraq, Syria, Libya, Somalia, Yemen, Sudan, Turkey, Palestine, Kashmir, Myanmar, Columbia, Honduras, Mexico and the Philippines. The red horse, like the red star, is blood and the blood is warm and the shallow flesh and the quivering bone come alive through the sacred light flowing from the ample, luminous lips of the hot crimson planet of evening. Through it, the entire weapons industry will come to heel as the CEOs and board members and major share holders of each of the major weapons manufacturers in this country and abroad are hunted down and executed.

The black horse, the great sable stallion of the

south, will throw and trample the rider who is Famine, those who control the production of and horde food from the masses in east and southern Africa, Guatemala, Somalia and North Korea. The black horse, like the black star, is shade and the shade is now and the burning skin and the wasted mind are moistened in the not hot, not cold lotion of ageless wisdom hidden in the heart of the velvet black planet of midnight. Through it, the entire agriculture industry will come to heel as the CEOs and board members and major share holders of each of the major seed engineering and fertilizer manufacturers in this country and abroad are hunted down and euthanized.

The white horse, the great snowy stallion of the north, will trample the Beast that is Pestilence. It will trample those who manufacture and deliver SARS, HIV, AIDS, ebola and zika. The white horse, like the white star, is time and time is an illusion and the sweeping hand and the half turned stone are stilled and cracked by the sand ladened wind in the ice chilled sigh of the white tranquil planet of dawn. Through it, the entire pharmaceutical industry will come to heel as the CEOs and board members and major share holders of each of the major drug manufacturers in this country and abroad are hunted down and slain.

The pale yellow horse, the great ocher stallion of the east, will trample the rider who promotes and profits from death, and who *is* Death, generating economic chaos within and between countries so that he alone may benefit. The pale yellow horse, like the yellow star, is mind and the mind is cold and the brazen ego and the withering id are fed and bled by the jagged teeth in the analytic mouth of the iced amber planet of noon. Through it, the entire financial industry will come to heel as the CEOs and board members and major share holders of each of the major financial instruments trading firms on Wall Street and abroad as well as the heads of all the central banks are hunted down and killed.

The horses will rise up in concert and in a herd and trample the horsemen and all their henchmen far and wide, high and low. The horses will run with breakneck speed through the lush, black low lands and the yellow and red high plains, through the cold, white snows, the warm, wet marshes, the hot, powdery sands, through cobblestone towns and

Larry Redmond

villages as well as welded steel cities. The horses will run everywhere trampling the Beasts who once rode them and thought they were their own.

I know this because I am the herdsman and the whisperer. It is I, not the riders, who hold the reins and the crop. For I am God, and I control the horses. I am the wrangler, and I will unleash the power of the white and red and black and yellow horses. They've spent too long in the belly of this hell created by the beasts and now they shall run in unison and be free. They will live like they were meant to live, like God intended for them to live. They will live like what they are. They will live like horses.

III

The morning following my run-in with Reverend Milton, I was awakened by someone pounding on my front door. After our last job, everybody in the crew split up and traveled to different parts of the world until the heat subsided. Brit went to London, and Jiqin went to Rio. I had not expected any company until one or both of them returned. They would only be gone for a few months, but at the moment, I was alone. I didn't know where the other guys went, but none of them even knew where I lived, let alone would be making an unannounced visit. The pounding came again at the front door.

I struggled up and stumbled to the living room. I looked out the peephole. It was Ida. I couldn't imagine why she was here. I opened the door.

"Was that you?" she asked, stepping straight inside.

"Was what me?" I asked back.

"Don't play with me," she answered. "You know what."

I knew what she wanted to know. She was asking about the Cach twin killings. How did she even know about it? I couldn't get any news coverage on

27 Larry Redmond

it.

"I don't know what you're asking," I said, although I knew perfectly well.

"You seen the news?" she asked.

"No," I answered. "What's happened?"

"They're calling it the pharm stand killings," she said. "Pharm spelled with a 'ph,' not an 'f.'"

"And you want me to tell you what?" I asked.

"I want you to tell me if you did it."

"I didn't do it," I lied.

"You're a fucking lier."

Who did she think she was? I came within a split second of confessing just to spite her, just to show her I was a bad ass motherfucker. The living room still smelled of the sandalwood incense I had burned the night before while watching Perry Mason. Instead, I composed myself and said, "I hate to disappoint you." It was early, so shafts of sunlight streamed in the crack between the drapes at the front windows.

"There's a video circulating on Youtube," she said.

I tried to act nonchalant, but I think she saw straight through me.

"Have you seen it?" I asked.

I detected a hint of nervousness in my own voice.

"I've seen it," she said. "That's why I'm here."

"So, what's on it?"

"Everything," she said. "Somebody videotaped the whole thing. The faces are masked and blurred out, but it's all there."

"So who shot it?"

"That's the question the cops are asking." She paused for a moment, then said, "They're calling you guys heros."

"Who?"

"The folks who commented about the video."

"Heros?" I asked.

She shrugged saying, "They claim it was better executed than the Mumbai Taj hotel attack, because there was no collateral damage. The only people who died were members of the capitalist establishment. You should be proud." Then she asked, "Did you suffer any losses?"

"No," I answered. "We all got away."

Ida used to be fine. Well, actually, she still was. Just older is all. She aged well. I'm the one who aged like a piece of shit. Her skin was the color of roasted almonds. Her face was lean with high cheek bones and a pointed chin, and her large brown eyes looked as if they were placed on a slant like cat's eyes. Only now, she had vertical lines, one on each side of her mouth. The skin on her full nose and lips seemed darker than they used to be, maybe from too much sun or wind or harsh creams. The lids of her eyes were heavier than they used to be, and the outside corners drooped just a little mitigating that cat-eyed look. Her hair was white and cut close like a man's. It formed a half inch long layer of fuzz all over her head. It was so thin, I could see her scalp through it. I remember thinking that her head looked like a giant peach when I first saw this hairstyle some time ago. Her skin was weathered, but the young woman was still there staring at me over the distance of time. I could still see in her the young woman that had gotten her first natural and had joined the Black Legion years earlier.

"I guessed it was you in the tape by the way you moved," she said.

"But you weren't sure."

I guess I was hoping she wasn't sure, but she didn't bother to answer.

By now, she was sitting on the edge of the couch, her legs crossed at the ankles. After a few seconds, she relaxed and scooted all the way back onto her seat, and crossed one leg over the other at the knee.

"So who were the two women?" she asked.

I played her question off. "Just members of the team," I said. The question caught me by surprise, and I looked away. I pretended to be preoccupied with my books in the shelves next to the empty aquarium, with my swords on the walls across from the books, my burlap sack drapes, my black leather couch. The living room still had a hint of linseed oil mixed in with the sandalwood. I yawned to indicate to her that I wanted to go back to bed.

"You must have had a dozen people," she said finally.

"Close," I said. I yawned again.

"And only two women?" she asked.

"They helped with the planning."

I guess she was trying to make it like it used to be between us, but it wasn't the same. We weren't in love any more, and being there with her bringing up that old feeling felt strained.

"So, did you come here to warn me?" I asked.

"Do I need a reason to come visit my husband?" she asked in return.

I was taken by surprise again. Yes, we were still married, technically. But we hadn't been together in years. And she was, after all, still crazy. At least, in my mind she was.

The only thing I could muster to say was, "That was a long time ago."

"Yes," she answered, "but some things don't die."

"My life is different now," I said.

"Your life is what it is because of me."

She was right, and I knew it. She's the one who got me involved in Black politics years ago when we were still living together. She had wanted me to join the Black Legion. I resisted, but she was adamant. When the police vamped on the Black Legion office and killed two of our closest friends along with their child, the two of us carried out a counter raid where we killed a couple of cops, and burned down the police station. Later, she's the one who introduced me to Aba, who, in turn, got me started in this business. She's the one who tipped me off about the now-deceased Israeli prime minister, Nathan Benjamin. It is because of her teachings that I wacked him.

"So, where are we going with this?" I asked.

"I want in," she answered.

"Is that a good idea?" I couldn't think of a graceful way to raise the question of how her mental health suffered after our first raid together. She had a breakdown that led to her being hospitalized for I didn't know how long.

"I can handle it," she said.

"How can we be sure?"

"There are no sure things in this life," she answered.

"Ida," I said, I had to lay it out, "I don't think you can deal with the killing."

"Let me worry about that," she said.

"No, I have to worry about that. The whole team would be at risk if you should falter."

"Is that your only concern?" she asked.

"Meaning what?" I asked back.

"I know about your girlfriends."

Jiqin and Brit were not on my mind, but I could not help wondering how Ida knew about them. I didn't want to look Ida in the eye, so I focused on the bits of dust floating in the shafts of sunlight between the drapes.

"You were gone for a long time," I said.

"But I'm back now."

"A lot has happened since you left."

"Did you divorce me?"

"No."

"Then it's still all good," she said. "I'm back healthy now, and I want to try to get you back in my life."

"My life is already full," I said.

"I'm not going to make it fuller," she said. "I'm your wife. I'm going to make it better."

She stood up and started towards the door. I stopped her before she could leave.

"I've changed a lot over the years," I said. "The folks I'm with now . . .."

She cut me off, "You mean your women. You can say it."

It was not as hard now as it used to be mustering the courage to say unpleasant things to Ida.

"My current women and I don't do the same kinds of things that you and I used to do." I tried to think of a euphemism for kinky. Nothing came to mind, so I just spit it out. "The stuff we do now is kind of twisted."

"You're twisted; I'm crazy. We'll see how that works out."

She left without closing the door behind her.

Crazy is a funny concept. Ida knocking on my door this morning brought to mind the lyrics of the El Dorados classic, At My Front Door.

Crazy little mama come knocking
Knocking at my front door, door, door
Crazy little mama come knocking
Just like she did before.

Thinking about the song pulled me into thinking about the notion of being crazy. Crazy TV Lenny came to mind. I recalled him giving away bicycles in order to lure people into his appliance stores. Maybe he should have been called Crazy Like a Fox TV Lenny. I wondered if Ida was being crazy like a fox.

I remembered the look in her eyes the night we torched that police station years ago. The whole scene began to replay itself. I could see again the frosted glass doors as I pushed them open and peeped in. The desk sergeant, a gaunt man with large brown eyes and thinning hair, stood up and asked, "May I help you?" Another officer who was seated by the desk with his back to the door turned to see who I was. They were both wearing their uniform blues. I stepped in, leveled the Remington I carried at the desk sergeant and fired twice. He dropped. The younger officer jumped up and reached for his revolver, but not fast enough. I emptied my rifle into his chest. Just then, a third officer opened a frosted glass door on the other side of the room. Ida pointed her rifle at him and fired. The bullet struck him in the shoulder. It only slowed him a little as he reached for his gun. I remembered that I shouted, "in the head!" Ida fired three quick shots. The first two missed, but her third shot plunged into his left eye kicking blood and bits of flesh into its wake. His right knee buckled and he dropped his gun. A puddle of thick red blood gathered around his head when he hit the floor. Ida dropped her piece and stared at him.

Did she look crazy then, or was she merely reflecting the crazy she saw in me?

After locking the door behind her, I headed back towards the bedroom. I wasn't done getting my rest. I was just about to detour into the bathroom to take a leak when there came a knocking on the door again. I checked the peephole. It was Ida again.

"Did you forget something?" I asked through the door.

"We need to talk," she answered.

"About what?"

"About you."

I opened the door and stood back against the wall. She barged in and sat down in the same spot as before.

"You're a natural," she said. "I saw it that night after we shot up those cops. You are a natural-born killer."

"You came back to tell me that?"

"No," she answered. "I came back to tell you that I am one, too. That's what drove me crazy for all those years. I couldn't come to grips with who and what I was."

"Now you can?" I asked.

"Yes, I can," she said.

"You've proven yourself?"

"Yes, I have," she answered.

"How?" I asked.

She looked me in the eye with an unflinching stillness.

"Brit and Jiqin won't be coming back."

I think she was waiting for me to react, but I stayed cool. Granted, I had not talked with them in a few days. That was part of the plan. No communication for three months.

"Okay," I said, "I'll bite. Why won't they be coming back?"

"They are how I have proven myself," she answered.

"You killed Jiqin?" I asked.

The notion of Ida having killed Jiqin was ridiculous. Jiqin was herself a trained killer, one of the best. Ida may have been able to sneak upon Brit and take her out, but there was no way she could match Jiqin. I allowed myself the luxury of a smile in order to avoid bursting out into raucous laughter.

"You think I'm lying, don't you?" she asked.

"I don't know if you're lying or not," I replied. "I just know that Jiqin is a professional, and would be very difficult to kill."

"Even professionals have weaknesses," she said.

I thought about it for a moment and asked, "Where did all of this happen?"

"Rio," she answered. "It all went down in Rio." It sounded crazy, but no one was even supposed to know that Jiqin was in Rio. I wondered how Ida knew.

"You know I can simply call her," I said.

"Yes," she said, "I know." She paused for a long moment, then said, "So call her."

I did. I got a message that said the number I was trying to reach was no longer in service. I couldn't remember if we decided to all get new cell phones.

"Her phone is no longer in service," I said.

"I think I threw it into the Amazon River," she answered.

I wasn't as much worried as anxious to get Ida's lie exposed. For some reason, I thought that proving that Jiqin was still alive would put an end to this lie, and also demonstrate once and for all that Ida was in fact still crazy.

"Do you want me to tell you how I did it?" she asked.

"No," I answered, "don't bother." I was so certain Jiqin was still alive, I did not want to hear Ida spinning some fantastic yarn. I feigned another yawn, and complained about wanting to get more sleep.

"You get some sleep, baby," she said. "I'll be right here when you wake up."

Leaving Ida in the living room, I took a piss, then slipped back into bed. I did not sleep, though. I could not help wondering if maybe Jiqin was dead for real.

39 Larry Redmond

IV

Being picked on as a kid was a motherfucker. This was back in the day when school yards were filled with gravel, and running and especially sliding in the gravel were a game in itself. I was fast, the second fastest boy in my class. The first fastest boy, who had the same first name as me, could always beat me. He was bigger than me, more muscular. And he had a big, round head like a bowling ball. He liked me, because I was the only one who gave him any competition when we played.

I was smarter than he was. Or maybe he just believed the bullshit about Black boys being dumb, and I didn't. He always cut me some slack in the playground, because he respected my intellect. I never figured out why. It wasn't like I was helping him with his homework or anything like that. Back then, boys who were smart just got respect. Well, sometimes.

He was also kind of a protector. He looked out for me, gave me a heads-up if he thought I needed it. Some boys resented other boys being smart. Or maybe I just looked like a punk that other boys wanted to beat up on.

I had other protectors, boys– and girls– who were willing to fight bullies on my behalf. I was always fascinated by the way my protectors fought. It was like a dance. They would bounce, shifting their weight from one foot to the other while modulating their fists up and down together in unison from in front of their face to in front of their chest, shifting their weight to one foot as their fists went up and shifting their weight to the other foot as their fists went down. Their opponents would do the same or a similar dance, then someone would swing, and it would turn into a cat fight, arms swinging like windmills. After a few blows were landed, it would be over, usually.

One fight I remembered lasted for almost five minutes. Two girls fought over I knew not what, and after the windmill swinging, they grabbed each other's hair and each tore the other's blouse off. After a while, they simply got tired and stopped and staggered away. One of the girls had her bra ripped as well. She staggered away covering her almost black, melon-like breasts by holding the pink rag that had been her blouse over her chest.

Nobody ever showed me how to fight, so I thought the dance was the way it was supposed to be. It was

41   **Larry Redmond**

years before I learned that the dance was merely for show, to make you look tough, and that real fighting had nothing to do with the dance.

Back then, the Chicago public school system didn't automatically promote students who got poor grades. So there were a lot of people who were in the sixth grade who were much older than me, maybe by as much two, three or more years.

One young man, and he was a man, sat right next to me. I think they put him next to me so I could be a positive influence on him, make him want to learn. But he had been to Korea. So there was nothing that *I* could teach *him*. He would come to school smelling like after-shave lotion. That's how I knew he was a man. We became friends, sort of. He would tell me stories about the war, and I was always eager to hear them.

He was one of the tallest people in the class, because he was one of the oldest. He was dark with thick muscles at the base of his jaw. The skin along the ridge of his jaw was covered with razor bumps. His nose was broad and flat, his eyes bulbous and sad.

He told me once that he and his buddy in Korea at the time began digging a foxhole. The problem was that they began digging in a grave site. Of course, they didn't know it was a grave site until they got down a couple of feet into the ground. Before they could get out and scout out another site, the enemy began firing on them. They were forced to live in a hole with corpses for a week. One night, one of the corpses groaned. He said it scared him half to death. But he couldn't leave, because leaving the foxhole would have meant getting shot. So, he had to suck it up.

He told me that story after I came to my seat, and found him with his head down on his desk crying. He wiped the moisture from his sad eyes with a brusque swipe of his hand. A week later, he dropped out of school completely. He said he needed to find a job. About a week after that, I saw him hanging around the playground with some other older boys. I tried to speak to him, but he ignored me. He didn't want his friends to know that he had a friend who was a child. I never saw him again after that.

One day, a boy I had never seen before bumped into me in the playground. He took umbrage as if *I* had bumped into *him*. He was short and pudgy with fat jowls and stubby fingers. He started doing the

fight dance, and told me to "go for what you know."
I didn't know what he meant. And since I didn't
know how to do the fight dance, I just stood there.

"Go for what you know," he said again.

I looked around to see if my running partner was
anywhere nearby, but all I saw was the crowd
gathering to see the fight. I felt sick. My stomach
began to churn. I knew I was good at drawing
things, but I couldn't figure out how to work that
knowledge into this situation. I began pondering
what other things I knew that I could use right then
when another one of my classmates came to my
rescue. A girl– a young woman actually– asked me
if I wanted her to take care of this for me. She was
buxom and tough and looked old enough to be
somebody's mother. What I remembered most
about her was that her hair was 'going back.' I
nodded in the affirmative. She didn't bother doing
the fight dance. And when *he* did the fight dance,
she just took off after him, hitting him around his
head and shoulders as if she were shooing away
mosquitoes. He took off running. I never saw him
again after that, either.

Eventually, I got to see what "go for what you
know" really meant. I had a run-in with another

playground bully. He was taller than me and skinny and had light skin with acne pimples on his forehead. He had grayish-green eyes. He didn't bother to use the pretext of me bumping into him. He simply wanted to fight. In the half second before he began the dance, I stuck my hand out to shake hands, hoping to quell the situation. It didn't work.

"Go for what you know, punk," he said.

He swung at my head. I ducked and wheeled around and ran. He chased me, but I was too fast for him. I ducked into the local neighborhood bakery, but the owner, a skinny white woman with a beak nose and blue eye makeup, quickly whisked me back out, and closed up shop.

Ducking into the bakery had been a bad idea, because it allowed my attacker to almost catch me at the bakery door after the owner put me back out. Once out, I began to run again. At this point, I had not learned that I was invincible, so I used the only weapon I had. I ran. I ran as fast as I could. Seeing that he couldn't catch me, he stopped chasing. I didn't stop, though, until I was all the way home.

Larry Redmond

V

"You guys went after the wrong target."

Ida was sitting on the edge of the bed.

"What time is it?" I asked.

"Noon," she answered. "You slept a lot."

"What are you doing in here?" I asked. I had left her in the living room.

"We need to change our focus," she answered.

I wanted to get up and take a leak, but I felt uncomfortable getting up in front of her.

"Can I get some privacy for a minute?"

"I've seen your dick before," she said. "Many times."

I threw the covers off with a flourish and strutted around the bed to the bathroom. Ida stared at my dick all the while.

"It's not a big as I remembered," she said.

I brushed my teeth and showered. As I pulled my undershorts on, Ida asked, "Aren't we going to consummate?"

"No," I said, "I am not going to fuck you."

"I don't want you to fuck me. I want you to make love to me."

"Let me see if I understand you correctly," I said.

"You go off and kill both my girlfriends, and now you want me to love you. Is that what I'm hearing?"

"I want you to love me, because I'm you wife," she said.

I needed to find a way to confirm Ida's story without her knowing about it. I needed her to give me some details.

"Okay," I said. "How did you do it?"

"Oh," she answered. "Now you want to verify that they're dead."

"Yes, I want proof."

"Why don't you believe me?" she asked.

"Because I don't believe you're that strong."

Almost as if on cue, the light coming in the bedroom window from outside began to fade and the brightness in Ida's face began to change to sadness. I walked over to the windows, and let the shades up. The view of Lake Michigan between the buildings across Sheridan Road always lifted my spirits, even on cloudy days. Today was not one of those days, though. Today, there was merely a single cloud drifting over the sun. After only a few seconds, as the cloud floated on its way, the brightness of the afternoon returned. The lake water looked deep bluish-green with small whitecaps rolling in.

Larry Redmond

"You hurt my feelings," she said.

"Ida," I said, "you have been in and out of the crazy house for years because you killed one cop a thousand years ago. Why would I now believe that you are somehow miraculously stronger?"

She looked towards the floor and turned her head away.

"Look at it from my point of view," I said. "If you killed my two girlfriends in order to get me back, you're crazy. If you lied about killing my two girlfriends in order to get me back, you're equally crazy." I paused for a moment, then asked, "So, which is it? Did you kill them, or did you lie?"

"I lied," she said.

"But why?" I was simultaneously relieved and furious. "What could you possibly have gained by pulling a stunt like that?"

She snapped back, "I wanted in."

"Why didn't you just ask?"

"I didn't think you would believe me or trust me."

She was right. I wouldn't have. But this stunt *did* get my attention.

"How did you know Jiqin was in Rio?" I asked.

"I hacked you computer," she answered. "I knew the travel plans for your entire crew. I knew both she and Brit were not planning to be back for several months. I was hoping to use that time to make you change your mind about me."

"I guess I'd better get rid of that computer," I said.

"No need," she answered. "I scrubbed it for you."

"So now what?"

"Let me pick your next target," she answered. "Right now, your picks are too random."

"You don't know what we're after," I said.

"Yeah, I do. You're killing billionaires in order to crash the system for the benefit of the people."

Well, she did hit our goal right on the head.

"So, who should we be targeting?" I asked.

"The way you're going at it is no better that those people in the Middle East killing random strangers," she said, "and killing them by the hundreds. It creates terror in the general public, but those deaths won't sway the people you need to reach. In fact, you're doing them a favor by killing off a few peasants that they would kill themselves given the opportunity."

"The jihadists are wrong?" I couldn't believe I was asking that question.

"They got the right idea," she continued, "but like you, they go after the wrong targets. They clearly have no coordinated strategy or plan of attack. Right now, they're relying on sleeper cells to pick soft civilian targets of opportunity to exploit. That injures their cause, not helps it. Not that they care, but it creates ill will against them and their cause. Ironically, it helps the ruling elite in two ways. First, it reduces the population. It kills a couple of jihadists, *and* it kills scores of peasants at the same time. The attacks in Paris and London were perfect examples. For the ruling elite, those were win-win situations.

"But secondly, and more importantly, it gives them an excuse to impose more security and surveillance measures worldwide. The folks they and you need to kill are the families who own Bank of America, Citigroup, JP Morgan Chase and Wells Fargo as well as Exxon Mobil, British Petroleum, Royal Dutch/Shell and Chevron Texaco. If you want to change something, you need to reach *them*. *They* are the ones running the show, and *they* are the ones you need to target, the Rothschilds of Paris and London, the Goldman Sachs, the Rockefellers, the Lehmans and Kuhn Loebs of New York, the Warburgs of Hamburg, the Lazards of Paris, and the Israel Moses Seifs of Rome."

"That's a pretty tall order," I said.

"Freedom ain't free, and revolution ain't easy," she countered.

"Are any of the clowns Masons? I asked.

"Yes," she answered, "they all are."

VI

One day in gym class, we were running around in a loose free-for-all, playing whatever game each separate group of boys wanted to play, wrestling, tag, dodge ball.

It never ceased to amaze me the variety of tools our gym teacher would come up with from one session to the next. Usually, it would be balls for various games, basketball, volley ball, football. Sometimes it would be beanbag or dodge ball. But this particular day, he came up with fencing foils. Oddly enough, most of us wanted the usual balls and ropes. Only a few of us wanted to fence. Well, we didn't actually want to fence. We wanted to act out scenes we had seen in Errol Flynn movies.

My fast-running protector and I each grabbed one. We even knew the music. I guess we had both seen Captain Blood and heard Erich Korngold's score. We found a far corner, and faced off. He thought that because he was faster than me, he would win the dual. And he was almost right. Neither of us knew what we were doing, so we simply reenacted some of the moves we had each seen in that or a similar movie. We eased around the floor, striking poses and lunging, then climbed the gym's bleachers which had become the rigging of a triple-masted 17th century war ship. We hopped from one level to the next, up and down, posing and lunging, parrying and evading. We scat sang the musical score as we dueled, becoming louder and faster at especially dramatic moments.

Before long, we began to tire. That's when he decided to come in for the kill. I stumbled backwards, and he lunged. I parried, and counter lunged, still regaining my balance, the music fast and fiery. I could see the disappointment in his face as he felt my lunge strike home in his chest, but he knew how the game was played. He immediately adopted the role of the dying swordsman. He staggered down the aft deck holding his chest, flipped over the starboard railing, and fell into the sea. Then he hopped up and ran off to play volley ball.

Triumphant, I stepped off the last bleacher bench with a swagger. I was still Captain Blood. I must have stepped in the path of this boy who had been working out with a medicine ball. I remembered seeing him earlier on admire his own physique as he moved the medicine ball from his left side to his right and back again. He hoisted it over his head several times. I also remembered seeing him admire himself on those days when we had swimming. He would stand and pose at the edge of the diving board just before doing a swan or a jackknife. I stepped in his way, and he pushed me as he walked away. Captain Blood followed him and pushed him back.

That boy, clearly one of those who had been held back at least once and who had muscles cut like a bodybuilder, balled up both his fists, and hit me three times in the ribs and abdomen. He folded me over like a cardboard box. I was completely unable to breathe. I staggered backwards, struggling for air. My wobbly legs backed me into the wall next to the climbing bars where I promptly sank to the polished wooden floor and passed out cold.

I was surprised to learn that being knocked out was the same as being knocked asleep. The gym teacher waking me up was exactly like my mother waking me up in the morning. I might have even been dreaming. So, when I opened my eyes, I was surprised to see that I was still in gym class. I had expected to see my room, my bed, my blankets, my pajamas. I even felt rested, and I had no immediate memory of having just had my ass kicked.

After seeing that I was okay and telling me to sit there for a while and rest, the gym teacher left. That's when my fencing partner ran up and leaned over me.

"What did you hit him back for?" he asked, smiling sheepishly. His teeth were perfect. He had a sizeable gap in front between two pearly incisors.

I didn't realize it until that moment, but I still couldn't breathe properly. I could breathe, but I couldn't talk. I couldn't say it, but the answer was that it seemed like the right thing to do. He pushed me, and I pushed him back. That he then knocked me out cold did not even figure into it. It was the right thing to do, and I did it. In retrospect, maybe I should have been a little more cautious. They say everybody has twenty-twenty hindsight, but I'm not sure that's true. I'm not sure that I would not have done the same thing all over again, given the chance, despite the fact that it would be years before I would discover how powerful I truly was.

VII

I needed to talk to Menachem. The trouble was, I had no way to reach him. Menachem and I had established a relationship when I went to Israel to kill the Antichrist, Nathan Benjamin. At the time, Benjamin was the Prime Minister of Israel, so I needed some help getting it done. Menachem was the one who helped me. Ultimately, he was the one who set it up, because he had access to resources in Israel that I did not have. So, I ended up as just the trigger man.

During our conversations together, he vehemently argued that it was the Masons who were running the country in Israel. He also pointed out that the same Masons were running America. At the time, we didn't know who those Masons were, so we settled on killing billionaires at random, since billionaires were the ones who benefitted from the economic chaos being wreaked upon the masses. Our arrangement was that he would pick the targets and I would do the hits. Menachem was the one who pointed out that the entire board of directors and the largest investors of the Cach twins' pharmaceutical manufacturing company needed to die, not just the twins themselves. We then formulated and executed the actual plan of attack.

"This is one of those companies that supplied both sides during World War II," he had reasoned, his baritone voice low and melodious, "selling chemicals to the Nazis to manufacture gas, and chemicals to the Allies for medicine. Their entire board of directors needs to die." Thinking back on it, I often thought that he should have been a singer.

But now that Ida had named the top eight families in the world as the ones responsible for the misery mankind was suffering, I thought Menachem and I should renegotiate our arrangement.

The system of communication we had worked out was that he would send me a secure phone by way of diplomatic channels, then I would call him. After our conversation, I would destroy the phone. The system worked well. The only problem with it was that I had no way of reaching out to him. I was forced to wait.

It took six weeks. During that time, Ida lived with me. She was homeless. Apparently, over the years, she had spent a lot of time being homeless, times when she was released from the looney bin– her words, not mine– but had no place else to go. Many of our conversations related to our experiences living on the streets, the shelters we went to, the free kitchens we ate at. It turned out that she spent a lot of time at the Salvation Army over on Clark Street. She had a room there. She knew Reverend Milton.

"Biggest asshole on the planet," she said. "Always trying to fuck somebody."

"I thought he was pretty honest and straight forward," I said in his defense.

"I don't mean fuck *over* somebody," she came back. "He spent years in prison, so he was always trying to catch up on all the pussy he missed out on."

The first couple of weeks she lived with me, the environment was pretty formal. I told her she could sleep in the living room, and I gave her some sheets and blankets and towels, which she rolled up every morning, and stored behind the couch.

She was on SSI, Supplemental Security Income, because she was old and crazy. So she got a small check every month to buy stuff. I was tempted to simply give her some money, but then I thought better of it. I didn't want her to think we were married for real. She didn't have much in the way of clothes, so she went to one of the local second-hand stores, and bought some. I think she thought that if she had lots of clothes in my house, it would help establish her residency there.

At first, she was storing her clothes behind the couch with her bedding. But after about two weeks, I would find some of her shit stored in the linen closet. That's about the time she started not tying her bathrobe as tightly as she had been a day or two earlier. I pretended not to notice the fullness of her ample bosom and brown belly. I simply looked the other way.

Looking the other way worked for about a day. After that, she began brushing by me ever so lightly wheneve we were in close quarters.

"I'm sorry," she would say. "I don't know why I keep bumping into you."

I would make some nondescript utterance, and acknowledge that the contact was indeed an accident.

The final straw came about three weeks in. She walked into the kitchen completely naked, yawning.

"Oh," she said, "I didn't know you were up yet." She folded her arms over her breasts to conceal them. I stepped to one side to get around her, but, feigning an accident, she stepped that same way. I stepped to the other side, and she did the same. Feigning exasperation, she fell into me, her naked breasts brown and full against my T-shirt. She looked up at me, then looked away sheepishly.

"I'm so sorry," she said. "You must think . . .."

"It's okay," I answered.

I eased by her, careful not to touch anything, and escaped to my bedroom.

The next few days were uneventful. I went down to the Green Mill to see if Milton was still playing there. He wasn't. I took a couple of walks by the beach. I waded in the surf a couple of times, enjoying the cool water on my feet and ankles, and the feel of the pebbles and sand on the underside of my toes and arches and heels. I spent some time trying to figure out when was the last time I had heard from Menachem. It was before the pharm stand hit, but that didn't help me much. The real question was when was he going to send another phone. Since there was no connection between the time between calls and the calls themselves, knowing when the last call was proved worthless.

In truth, talking to Menachem was pointless. There was no law that said I had to wait for him to do a job. If Ida had a reasonable game plan, I could and would simply go with it.

Ida spent those few days shopping. Every day, she scoured secondhand stores for clothes. Every day, she returned with bags full of plaid and flower print dresses, striped skirts, pink and yellow and red blouses, black and brown leather shoes, dark green and black felt hats, navy blue and coffee brown coats, ripped denim jeans, tan wool slacks and accessories, shell necklaces, brass bracelets, silver colored earrings, elastic belts, new underwear, panties, bras, tights, socks. One whole side of the living room was taken up with Ida's new clothes.

"You must be spending a fortune," I said.

"This was fifty cents," she answered holding up a jade-looking bracelet. "This was a dollar," she said holding up a lime green skirt.

She appeared to be warming to her topic, and I didn't want to hear all those prices, so I got right to the subject.

"What's you game plan?" I asked.

"I was thinking of getting something for every season," she answered. "Especially winter. I'm always underdressed in winter."

"Wrong game plan," I said.

"Oh," she said. "You mean what's my plan of attack."

"Exactly. What is your plan of attack?"

"That is going to cost you."

"Cost me what?"

"Letting me in."

"I can't let you in, Ida. That is a call the whole crew has to make."

I was lying. I could make the call. I just didn't want to do it.

"But you could make a recommendation," she said.

"Yes, I could."

"So, make the recommendation."

"I'll have to think about it."

"Then I'll have to think about giving my plan of attack."

I thought about it for a moment, then asked, "If I let you in, will you follow orders?"

"Of course I will," she answered.

I wanted to believe she was lying, but she seemed genuine. I tried to remember whether she had been a good liar when we lived together years ago. Nothing came to mind.

"So, is that it?" She asked, "Am I in?"

"I'll sleep on it," I answered.

A phone arrived the very next day. The packaging was the same, but different somehow. I couldn't put my finger on it, but something wasn't right. I opened it, and placed the call. A woman answered. She said, "Hello."

When Menachem and I set this phone exchange plan up, the idea was to limit who knew anything about what we were doing. The fact that Menachem did not answer was a problem. It meant that our plan had been compromised. I disconnected the call. I tried to open the phone to destroy the chip, but it was sealed tight, literally glued into one solid piece of plastic. I had to get it out of the house. Apparently, someone didn't want this phone to be easily opened. That meant it probably had some kind of homing chip in it, something to let someone know where it was. I had to get this thing out of the house now.

Ida walked into the room just as I was preparing to leave. She was about to ask where I was going, but I put my finger to my lips to hush her. She caught right on. She looked at the phone and instantly knew the danger we could be in.

She went over to her pile of clothes, and fished

around for something. From under the pants pile, she withdrew a copper box. She opened it and emptied its contents, all her necklaces, earrings and bracelets. They formed a heap on the floor that looked like a take from treasure island, golden and glittery. I put the phone in the box, and she replaced the top. From under a different part of her stash of clothes, she pulled out a roll of duct tape. We sealed the box, and both headed out to dispose of it. We walked a few blocks west and a few blocks north, and dropped the box into a dumpster behind a restaurant. When we got back to the building, there were two dull grey Chevy SUVs in the driveway. Men with close haircuts and dark glasses climbed out and headed into the vestibule.

Just like that, we were on the lam. Luckily, Ida was like me. We were both accustomed to life on the streets. We needed to find a place for the night. I had money, because we had just done a job. Menachem had financed it. There was plenty left over. That money was what allowed members of the crew to vanish overseas for months. Ida and I were homeless, but we were not on the streets.

"We need to leave the north side," Ida said.

"We need to rethink everything," I countered.

I tried to remember what I might have left in the apartment that could identify me, connect me with anything. I was pretty confident there was nothing. As a routine, I removed all potentially incriminating stuff, and stored it off site. My initial plan had been to leave the country for a few months like the rest of the crew. I didn't know what possessed me to keep that apartment, anyway.

I had to assume Menachem was compromised or dead. Either way, he was permanently out of the picture. Too bad. I already missed his insights into world history.

"Hitler is a prime example," he had said once, "of the damage the Masons can cause."

"Was Hitler a Mason?" I had asked.

"Not that I know of," he had answered. "He was simply one of their victims. Like Lincoln and the Czars of Russia before him and Kennedy after him, Hitler tried to divorce his country's economy from the Rothschild's banks. Hitler issued his own money, and built the strongest economy in Europe by having his people build the German infrastructure, roads, the Autobahn. When Hitler started killing Jews, it wasn't racism."

"But he was a racist," I had cut in. "I've read *Mein*

Kampf."

"Yes," he agreed, "but in this instance, he was trying to get back at the Rothschilds and other Jewish bankers. It was always about the money."

Thinking about that conversation now, I wondered why he didn't have us target a Rothschild. Then I remembered. He *did* want us to target one. But I think we had already settled on the Cach twins. I needed to know more about Hitler.

First and foremost, I needed to buy a van, something Ida and I could sleep in, and have something to get around in. I also needed to buy it from a private person, so I wouldn't have to fill out any kind of application. I checked Craigslist. I found a cargo van for $3,000. I called the number using a burner phone. The guy seemed nice enough. He wanted to meet in the park at 87th and Western. Cash only. We agreed to meet at noon the next day.

Ida and I spent that night in a cheap hotel using false names. She sat naked in front of the TV massaging her feet. I pretended not to notice, but it was a fake. She saw that I couldn't take my eyes off her, so she angled herself to make her pussy clearly visible as she ran her fingers between her toes, then squeezed them. She was clearly becoming aroused, because I could smell her pussy within seconds. Desperate to not succumb to her pressure, I turned in early. Once in bed, I pretended to fall asleep with her spooned behind me. It was difficult smelling her and feeling her breasts on my back and feeling her flex her hips gently against my butt, but eventually, I fell asleep for real.

The next day, we arrived at the park a few minutes early. I wanted to make sure no one was around to witness this purchase. The road into the park was off Western Avenue, and curved slightly north further in. We found a green picnic table close to the entrance, and waited.

Right on schedule, a white van pulled into the parking lot. The driver, a young, dark-complexioned white boy wearing a blue New York Mets baseball cap, looked around the area as he pulled the van to a slow stop. I had an uneasy feeling about the way he was looking around, so I immediately approached the driver side door.

"This looks like a nice truck," I said.

"Yo," he said, "it runs real good."

I thought he was trying to sound like a brother. He stepped out.

"Looks to me to be worth more than what you are asking."

He was a big kid, about six feet two inches, wearing a New York Mets uniform shirt. Darryl Strawberry, number 18. The shirt was out over his pants. He casually stepped back a couple of paces while looking back over his shoulder. I knew he was increasing the gap between us in order to pull a weapon. I closed that gap as soon as he reached for his pocket. Realizing he had lost the element of surprise, he tried to yank the pistol out quickly. As soon as the handle cleared his pocket, I grabbed his wrist and stomped on his foot with all my weight. He instantly lost his balance, and I used that moment to reach around and grab his little finger to pry his hand off the gun. But he was quick, and he was strong. He caught his balance, and snatched away. The gun went off. The bullet popped into the black pavement.

"Get off me, motherfucker," he screamed as I charged in and grabbed his wrist again.

This kid was dangerous, and I had to stop him. I hit him straight in his sternum with the heel of my open palm. He lurched backwards. He would have fallen back ten or twelve feet, except that I was still holding onto his wrist. He dropped to his knees. He pulled the trigger on the pistol until it was empty. Then he released it. He fell to the ground gasping for air.

I signaled to Ida. By now, she was behind the van to avoid getting hit by a stray bullet. She brought me the purse where she had stowed the money for the van. It was one of her secondhand bags, straw with pink and purple embroidered flowers. I snatched the bag from her, and threw it on the ground by his face.

"Here's your money," I said. "Thanks for the van."

As we drove from the park, I couldn't help but think that this was as inauspicious beginning.

The first stop was the nursing home to see Mighty Red. I needed to talk to her. I needed to know what she knew about Hitler.

At we approached the home, I noticed a big, dull grey Chevy SUV parked in front of it. It looked like one of the ones that were parked in front of the house yesterday. Not wanting to confront special agents from any governmental department, I pulled into the bus stop about half a block from the building. Ida noticed it, too.

"Who are these clowns, anyway?" she asked.

"I don't know," I answered. And I didn't.

After about 20 minutes, the same men with close haircuts and dark glasses that were at the house yesterday came walking out of the nursing home.

"This is not good," I said.

I wondered how they knew about Annie Miller. I had only recently discovered that she was even still alive.

Annie Miller a.k.a. Anna Müller a.k.a. Mighty Red was the woman who tried to kill me decades ago when I was stationed in Germany. She was a member of a religious group called *Das Innerste Feuer*. She thought I was the leader and prophet of a competing group called *Seiner Kinder*, and she wanted me dead because of who she thought I was.

I remembered how she turned Ruby, my wife at the time, against me. I could hear anew Ruby screaming "Anna-ah!!!" as loudly as she could years ago after I had discovered a sepia-colored picture of an individual that looked a lot like me. "Anna, he knows," she had cried out again. She thought that I knew who they thought I was. At the time, I did not. I would learn soon enough. Shortly thereafter, Mighty Red, attempting to kill me, stabbed Ruby in the chest and killed her instead. I was forced to desert the Air Force to avoid being charged with Ruby's murder.

It struck me as odd that I was on the lam then, and I was on the lam now. That's when it dawned on me that these guys could still be trying to solve Ruby's murder. But why now? What put them on my trail now?

Then it hit me! Mighty Red! The last time I visited her, I threatened to turn her in to the INS, and point out to them that she may have lied on her application for entry into this country. Her contacting the military about Ruby's murder was her way of fighting back. But how did she know where I lived? How did she know to send them to my house up on Sheridan Road?

I must have had a strange look on my face, because Ida broke my revery.

"Are you okay?" she asked.

"I'm fine."

"You don't look fine," she pressed. "You look like you've just seen a ghost."

"I have," I answered. "I have just seen the ghost of my . . .." That's when I realized that Ida didn't know about that part of my life. In that part of my life, I was Noel Bodie. Ida didn't come into my life until I became Al Pearsons. I pondered the notion of telling her the whole story about me. I couldn't remember whether or not I had told her that I was now Jay Sam Guy?

"Are we going in?" she asked, seeing the dull grey SUV pull away from the curb. There was a cloud of blue smoke trailing behind it. The damn thing was burning oil!

I was getting too old for this shit, all these different names and concealed identities.

"We can't see her today," I said. "There is something I have to do first."

"But I thought you were so hot-to-trot to question her about Hitler."

"I am," I said, "but not today."

I pulled the van out of the bus stop, and headed west in the direction of my storage locker.

VIII

It was the following day that the guard at the nursing home recognized me.

"Sherman," he said. "Right?"

I acknowledged that was my name. In fact, that was merely the name I had used the last time I came to visit her. It had been a variation of the dwarf's surname, Scheermann. He had been one of Mighty Red's goons back in Germany years ago. He's the one who shot me that day in Rainbow Park. It was through him that I found out Mighty Red was still alive and living in Chicago.

"I think she has lost it," he continued, shaking his head slowly from side to side. It was clear from his expression that he pitied her. "Ever since you left that last time, she keeps calling for somebody named Kwame."

"Aw, yeah," I said, not wanting to tip my hand that I had no idea who Kwame was.

He signed me in. I hadn't noticed it the last time I was here, but he wore a strong cologne, something spicy. The scent stayed with me half way down the hall.

When I reached it, I slipped into Mighty Red's

room as noiselessly as I could. She was lying in her bed. It had been months since I had visited her last. Apparently, she had taken a turn for the worst. I asked her how she was. She must have been hallucinating, because she began speaking to me in German at first. She knew I was there, but she didn't know who I was.

"*Auf Englisch, bitte,*" I whispered in her ear, hoping she wouldn't hear my accent or ask anything in German. I had hoped whispering would conceal my voice.

She hesitated for a moment. Maybe she didn't recognize my voice after all. But then she continued on, her voice barely audible.

"Is that you, Kwame?"

I had to make a split-second decision.

"Yes," I said.

She began to weep. It seemed odd watching this woman that I knew for a fact had been responsible for death after death after death in her earlier life actually lying there crying. My first thought was these have got to be crocodile tears. Then she took a deep breath.

"Oh, Kwame," she moaned, "why have you been gone so long?"

"I had business," I blurted out without even thinking. I almost called her baby. Then I remembered that I didn't know who Kwame was to her.

She stopped for a moment.

"You never had business before. What kind of business?"

I had to think fast again.

"I couldn't tell you about it before, because it was secret."

"Are you still working with the Reich?" she asked.

"Not anymore," I answered.

"What happened?"

"Things changed."

"Like what?"

"The war ended," I said. I paused for a moment. I needed to introduce the topic I wanted her to talk about, so I said, "Hitler died."

Her mood became somber. I was unsure of what to say to console her. I wanted to get her talking, but I didn't want to be too obvious. I decided to wait it out. I looked around her double-occupancy room. She still had no roommate. The pale grey curtain separating the beds was pushed all the way over to the pastel green wall. The room smelled of pine cleaner.

After a long moment, after she sniffed and wiped her eyes, she said, "I was a little girl, but I remember." She wiped her eyes again. "I remember the issues my parents discussed. The treaty of Versailles. The banks."

I could not help but recall Menachem discoursing on the problems Lincoln and Kennedy and the Romanovs had with banks in their times. My interest was piqued. I wanted to keep her talking. I knew this would be my last opportunity to get information from her.

"What about the banks?" I asked.

"Kwame," she said. The tone in her voice was strict. "We talked about this."

"I know," I said, "but tell me again."

"You're like a child wanting to hear the same story over and over again."

"You tell it so well," I said.

She ignored my compliment, and settled into her story.

"Hitler was a savior," she said. "After the war, . . ."

"The great war?" I interjected.

"Yes," she continued, "the great war. After that

war, Germany was in ruins. Germany was heavily in debt. It had to pay everybody's cost of that war." She sighed, then gave a little cough. She sniffed and continued, "Germany owed more money than all the land in Germany was worth. The Rothschilds wanted to lend Germany money, a loan that would have enslaved the German people forever." She sighed again. Then in a voice barely above a whisper, she said, "Hitler said, no. He was not going to allow his people to be enslaved."

"So, what did he do?"

"He printed his own money, Reich notes. And he bartered with other countries for goods, rather than dealing in money. He put people to work, rebuilding the country. He built the Autobahn. He built the peoples' car, the Volkswagen. He financed the research of Dr. Otto Warburg who discovered the only true cure for cancer. In five years from 1933 to 1938, he made Germany the most powerful country in Europe."

She paused a moment and smiled pondering Hitler's achievements. She was clearly proud of what he had done, but I was still back at someone having discovered a cure for cancer.

"A cure for cancer?" I asked.

"Yes," she answered.

"Who . . .," I couldn't think of how to finish the question.

"Dr. Otto Warburg," she answered as if my question were already fully formed in her mind. "He discovered that cancer cells generated energy by the fermentation of glucose, whereas healthy cells generated energy by oxidizing pyruvic acid. He discovered that cancer cells develop when there is a shortage of oxygen at the cellular level. His cure was simple. He developed a method of providing cells with adequate oxygen to prevent the fermentation of glucose, because fermentation only occurred when oxygen was lacking. That was the cure, but his banker relatives covered it up so they could continue making money from the sale of cancer treatments. His family wanted humanity to remain sick."

This was all news to me. I thought about all the cancer research I had done over the time that I knew Menachem. I never came across the name Warburg in that connection. The Warburgs were always the villains. Paul Warburg, after all, was one of the architects of the U.S. Federal Reserve Bank.

"When was this?" I asked.

"The early '30s," she answered. She paused for a long moment. *"Deutchland uber alis,"* she said finally. "I never told you this part," she continued, "but that had nothing to do with the idea of a master race." Her smile slowly faded. "It meant replicating the German economic system in every country in the world, minus the banking system as we know it, freeing the world from Rothschild and Warburg debt. It meant freedom for all humanity." Now her tone and countenance were somber again. She pressed her lips together until they were white to control her emotion.

"That's when the Rothschilds forced his hand. He didn't kill Jews because he thought they were inferior. He *was* a Jew!" she scoffed. "He killed them to get back at the Rothschilds and the Warburgs. They were killing his people, so he killed their people." She blew her nose and wiped her eyes. The pile of tissues on the floor by her bed was growing as she dropped each one after using it. "He was trying to save the world." She paused. "But people today think he was trying to conquer it." She closed her eyes. "He wanted to do in Russia what he had done in Germany, but the Rothschilds had to destroy Hitler and Germany in order to preserve their strangle-hold on the world banking system. That is why Hitler had to die."

I didn't say it out loud, but that was also why the Romanovs and Lincoln and Kennedy had to die. I was remembering Menachem, and wondering if we would ever work together again. Maybe we would if he wasn't already dead. She broke my train of thought.

"It was good in Germany back then," she said.

"How so?" I asked.

"What do you mean, how so? You were there!"

I scrambled for something to say, but nothing came to mind.

"*You* told *me* it was good in Germany back then," she said. "Or don't you remember?"

"I guess I don't remember," I mumbled.

"You don't remember?" Her voice was strict again. "How could you forget? You drove that big Mercedes all over the country, and the SS never gave you any trouble. Especially after the Olympics and Jessie Owens. That dark, African skin was magic back then." She harrumphed, then gave a small cough. "I remember all those women throwing themselves at you."

I took the chance that Kwame and Mighty Red

had been lovers when I said, "But it's you I loved."

She stopped in mid-sniff.

"You bastard," she said. "You never loved me. You just liked fucking me because my pussy was big enough to get that horse-dick of yours all the way in. And you liked humiliating that pipsqueak you called a wife."

I didn't know where she got the speed, but before I could react, she reached over and grabbed my crouch. Then as quickly as she had grabbed it, she let it go. She looked as if she was as surprised as I was. She paused for a long moment.

"You're not Kwame," she said at last.

She turned her head slowly in my direction. Then, for the first time since I arrived, she focused on me, on my face.

"Who are you?" she asked.

I didn't bother trying to hide my voice.

"Who were those men who were here earlier?" I asked.

"Who are you?" she asked again, this time clenching her teeth.

I didn't answer. Instead, I removed the small case from my pocket that I had retrieved from my storage locker. I opened the case and removed the vile.

Larry Redmond

"Who were those men?" I asked again.

"They are my protectors," she said. "I wish they were here now. They always brought cookies that I liked."

I removed the hypodermic needle. Keeping my back to the door so no one could see what I was doing, I filled the needle from the vile.

"You won't need them after today," I said.

"What have you done with Kwame?" she asked.

"Kwame died," I answered, "but he sent me to take care of you."

"He died years ago," she recollected, "from a heart attack."

"Let me massage your feet," I said. I placed the needle on top of the covers, in one of the natural folds.

"Kwame always did give a good foot massage." She smiled while shifting her feet and legs to the edge of the bed. "Did he teach you? What's your name, anyway?"

I moved to the far end, and grabbed both her feet, one in each hand. They were surprisingly warm. It seemed so incongruous that I was massaging the feet of the woman who tried to kill me way back when.

I rubbed the soles of her feet from the heel to the ball. I worked them with my thumbs, then squeezed her toes. She was so relaxed, her eyes began to droop.

"Your technique is not as good as his, but it's not too bad," she said.

I reached for the needle.

"Sherman!"

The voice was behind me. I knew from the scent of the cologne that it was the security guard from the front desk.

"I think she's dozing out," I whispered.

"She does that a lot," he answered. "That's one of the symptoms."

I palmed the needle, and slipped it into my pocket.

"Just as well," I said. "It's time for me to head out."

"I was going to ask if you wanted me to have the staff bring you anything," he said. "Some water? Some juice?"

"I'm straight," I answered. "Maybe next time."

I kissed Mighty Red on the forehead, and left.

Back in the van, Ida seemed in a pensive mood. I couldn't really give it any space, though. I had to figure out what our next move was going to be. I pulled away from the curb, and looked for some place to clear my head. I needed to think.

Ida asked, "Did you do it?"

"No."

"Why not? What happened?"

"The guard came in at the last moment."

She paused for a long moment before asking, "So, what's our next move?"

"I don't know," I answered, and I didn't.

IX

I needed to be alone so I could think. As it happened, Ida wanted to go for a swim that day, and I didn't. So I drove her over to Harris Park at 62nd and Drexel. I knew there was a pool there. I parked the van on the street, and gave her the key so she could have a place to crash after she swam. My plan was to ride the green line train for a while as I collected my thoughts.

She dug through her second-hand treasures, and came up with a pink, one-piece bathing suit studded with bright yellow sunflowers. It was absolutely hideous. She seemed to like it, though, so I smiled and waved as she pranced through the sliding glass doors into the building, her two-tone blue bath towel flung over her shoulder.

I walked the two blocks to the elevated green line stop at 63rd and Cottage Grove. I walked up the stairs to the platform and fished around in my pockets until I found money enough to pay for a ride. Once on the train, I sat back peering out the window at a group of young men below the station standing by the shops on the northwest corner of that intersection, their pants hanging low around their butts.

That's when I noticed an old man walking by them. He looked oddly familiar. He was blind, but he seemed to know where he was going, tapping the pavement ahead of him with his red-tipped, white cane. He tapped his way to the stairs leading up to the train platform. Within a few seconds, he was out of sight, hidden by the floor of the platform itself as the stairs led under it. I tried to figure out what was so familiar about him. Was it his gait, his build? I couldn't put my finger on it. And now that he was out of sight, I couldn't even remember what his gait and build were, so I stared back out over the intersection where the young men were still lingering.

Before long, I heard a tapping along the side of the train. It paused, then started up again, this time closer and moving in this direction. That's when I saw him, tapping along the side of the train car looking for the entrance. As he was about to step in, the doors began to close. I hopped up and blocked the door open with my shoulder so he could get in.

"Thank you, son," he said. "You've been a great service to an old man. I really didn't want to miss this train."

He was wearing a white dress shirt buttoned all the way up to his neck. It was frayed and yellowed at the collar and cuffs. He wore grey khaki pants with maroon suspenders and a black leather belt. His pants were pulled up to his rib cage. He looked like the comic-relief character in a sitcom television show.

"Let me help you find a seat," I said. I tried to grab his arm.

"No, no," he said. "Don't grab my arm. Let *me* grab *yours*."

I let him latch onto my elbow, and I led him to the seat where I had been sitting. He sat by the window, and I sat next to him.

"This seat is still warm," he said. "Is this where you were sitting?"

"It is," I said, "but don't worry about it."

"Well, thank you," he said.

There was a pause, then I asked, "How did you know I was a man before you heard my voice?"

"I could smell you," he said, "men and women don't smell the same."

As he sat folding his 4-section cane, and carefully tucking it away, I looked at his face. It was thin and long and dark. He had a one inch long scar at the

Larry Redmond

base of his jaw that had begun to keloid. He wore wraparound sunglasses to hide his eyes. His teeth were crooked and yellow. One of his upper front teeth was missing.

"So, what's your name, son," he asked.

"Folks call me Jay," I said.

"Well, my name is Adams," he said. "Wild Bill Adams from Texas."

"Glad to meet you, Wild Bill Adams from Texas," I responded.

The train began to pull away from the station, slowly at first, then gathering speed. We were both silent for a long moment, and I sensed that he had something on his mind.

"I get an odd feeling about you," he said at last, "but I can't put my finger on it."

"I'm not sure what you mean," I said. I decided not to mention that I had an odd feeling about him.

"Do I know you?" he asked.

"I'm sure we've never met," I said.

"I'm sure as well," he said, "but I can't shake this feeling. Maybe it's your voice."

"I don't know what to tell you," I said, all the while wondering why he seemed familiar to me.

"Tell me something about yourself," he said.

"Maybe that'll knock these cobwebs off my recollection."

"There's nothing to tell," I lied. The truth is, I didn't want to have to decide which of my personas to try to present to him. If he did know me, I didn't want to have presented the wrong persona to him. Having to explain that lie might be awkward. "I used to keep fish," I said at last.

"Did you now," he said. "What kind?"

"African cichlids," I answered. The blue one that I used to call Chuck came to mind. Chuck had been the bully of the 55-gallon tank I had before I headed off to Israel to kill Benjamin. He used to try to claim all the food in the tank for himself, but it never worked. The other fish simply circled around and fed while he wasn't looking or was too far away to respond quickly.

"African cichlids," Adams repeated to himself. "Aggressive little creatures," he said after a short pause.

"You know fish?" I asked.

"Oh, yeah," he answered. "I used to have a pet store in the Dallas area. I learned a lot about life watching the fish that I had for sale."

"They're pretty primitive," I said, thinking back

again about blue Chuck.

"Some of them are," he responded, "and some of them aren't."

To that notion I had no response, because the same could be said about anything.

"I learned how to live from a tiger barb," he said.

"And what did this tiger barb tell you?" I asked. I was being facetious, but he took it seriously.

"That fish taught me to live with reckless abandon."

"Is that the way to live?" I asked. "With reckless abandon?"

"Maybe reckless abandon is the wrong word," he admitted, "but certainly one should live without fear."

I thought about my own life, and the constant fear of having my true identity revealed.

Adams paused for a long moment, then asked, "Is Jay your real name?"

I couldn't answer. Was my fear being realized? No one had ever asked me that question before, and I was completely unprepared for it in this context, riding on a train with a total stranger who was blind.

"It's not, is it?"

I didn't answer.

"I didn't think so," he said. "You're a man of many secrets."

I looked back at his face, and I could see his eyes moving back and forth as if he were reading something very quickly on the inside of his glasses.

"I see it now," he said, "you're trying to change things, big things, but you're having doubts. You're thinking maybe it can't be done."

He clearly was seeing the doubts I was having the day before our last job. I had been fucking Jiqin and Brit at the time, but I was so riddled with doubt that I couldn't perform. I ended up rolling off them and crying. Maybe he was seeing vestiges of that doubt that I unwittingly harbored to this day.

"Changing the world is not easy," he said. "*Most* people think it cannot be done. But you *can* change it. You *will* change it. A lot of people think people who want to change things are crazy, because challenging the *status quo* is, in itself, crazy. But sometimes, that is what it takes."

I knew he was right. Challenging the *status quo* wasn't easy! Sometimes it requires that you commit murder.

Images of our last job flashed into my mind. I saw again the large oak trimmed conference room where

Cach Chemicals and Pharmaceuticals was holding its shareholders meeting. It was a large room with oil paintings of fat white men hanging on the walls. Some of these portraits were of men with pork chop sideburns and grey-tinged beards. I recalled that the Cach twins, who were both clean-shaven and parted their hair on the right side and had grey cowlicks, looked like they could have been a part of that collection.

Both twins wore glasses. The one I shot was taller than his twin, but not by much. I shot him in his chest just below his black bow tie as he flattened himself against the wall a few paces from the podium where he had just been speaking. Jiqin shot the other one, right in the forehead. Brit sprayed the audience with an Uzi hitting several of the major shareholders. Jiqin, Brit and I knew that what we were doing would be seen as crazy.

Wild Bill sat back and nodded slowly to himself. His lips were squeezed together tight. His eyes were relaxed behind his sunglasses.

I couldn't help but wonder how much he actually saw. Did he see the job we had just done? Did he see that I had shot one of the Cach twins myself?

"This is the story," he said suddenly, sitting

forward, "of the tiger barb and the oscar."

It was almost as if he were beginning to reveal to me his knowledge about my shooting one of the twins. I could feel myself becoming anxious.

"Back in my shop, I had a tank that I kept odds and ends in. The fish I put there usually didn't last very long. Sometimes, I would give them away. Sometimes, I would flush them down the toilet. This particular time, I had one lone oscar. I usually fed it goldfish. But this time, I wanted it to have to work for its dinner, so I put a couple of goldfish and a single tiger barb into its tank."

He sat back and paused in the telling of his story. It was as if he were examining his recollection for accuracy.

"I had expected the barb to hide behind the rocks I had strewn around the tank. But it didn't. It saw the oscar devour the goldfish, but it decided it was not going to live in fear. It darted out into the open water where the oscar could see it, and chase it. So the oscar obliged."

He turned his head in my direction as if for emphasis.

"At this point, I didn't know that the barb had made the decision it had made. I thought it simply hadn't discovered the obvious hiding places available to it. That's when it gave me the lesson."

Wild Bill sat forward again and weaved his open hands, the palms facing each other, back and forth, one over the other, to illustrate the tiger barb's movements.

"To escape the jaws of the oscar, it darted behind a large rock where it could have been safe for the rest of its life," he continued, "making only occasional excursions out for food. But it didn't stay there. It paused there for about five seconds panting. Then it darted back out into the open water again. Five seconds after that, it was still panting, but now it was in the oscar's mouth. I could see it in there looking out at the world for the last time, panting at the same rate it had been panting behind the rock. The oscar closed its mouth, made a couple of adjustments, then spit the barb's scales out its gills." Wild Bill sat back again. "The barb chose death over fear. *That* was the lesson it taught me, to not live in fear. And because of all the adrenaline in it at the time, it probably didn't even feel death when it came. Shortly after that, I lost my sight, but I never forgot that barb, and the strength of character it showed me. Crazy is as crazy does."

Wild Bill waited for the story of the tiger barb to fade. He waited for as long as a full minute, then said, "After Micah Xavier Johnson shot and killed five officers of the Dallas Police Department on Thursday, July 7, 2016, and wounded seven others, President Obama cast him as 'demented' and his motives as unknowable. Could we have expected anything different?"

He tilted his head as if he were listening for an answer. His voice, I noticed for the first time, was a high tenor that wavered as he spoke. I wondered what brought this up. How did Micah Xavier Johnson even come to his mind? Then he continued, "Dallas Police Chief David Brown said it might never be fully known why the 25-year-old former Army reservist snapped. Now, I looked for demented in Merriam-Webster. It was defined as 'not able to think clearly or to understand what is real and what is not real: crazy or insane.'"

Wild Bill cleared his throat, then continued, "It is obvious that Johnson's thoughts were crystal clear, and that he was able to understand what was real and what was not real. He articulated his goals and intentions with stunning clarity. His goal was to kill white people, especially white police officers. His intention was to get revenge for the killing of Black men by law enforcement personnel. Those were his words in plain English. What could be clearer than that?"

Wild Bill sat silent again for a moment, then said, "Micah Xavier Johnson was the tiger barb taunting the oscar. He knew what he was doing. He knew it was dangerous, and he was afraid. But the bottom line is that he decided to not live in fear. He swam out into the open water, and he let the oscar eat him."

Wild Bill angled his head in my direction.

"So," he said, "are you prepared to be the tiger barb in order to make the change you want to make? Are you prepared to let the oscar eat you?"

Once again, I didn't know how to answer.

X

"You know that the story of Adam and Eve is more than a tale of the fall of man, don't you?" Ida's tone was matter-of-fact, like she was telling something that, of course, everybody knew.

"I did *not* know that," I answered.

We were in the van getting ready to retire for the night. The van was idling while we arranged our stuff and ourselves. We had two sleeping bags and a small portable toilet by the rear doors that was our chamber pot. We had duffel bags with stuff we had gotten at various secondhand stores around town. Ida knew all the best places to shop.

She was sitting naked on top of her sleeping bag. We had a small flashlight for light. She knew I could see her scratching the hair around her pussy. She smelled the tips of her fingers, then continued scratching.

"The story of Adam and Eve is a cautionary tale," she said. "It has nothing to do with eating the apple, and everything to do with not trusting a snake."

"I think you've got the wrong story," I said.

"It's the exact *right* story," she said. "Only it isn't

about some fair maiden or trusting farmer getting bitten. It's about mankind being duped."

"I think I'm missing it," I admitted.

She stopped her story, and concentrated on her bottom.

"I need you to look at this for me," she said.

She scooted off her sleeping bag and onto mine. With her knees up, she spread her thighs as wide as she could get them.

"Do you see a pimple here?" She was fingering a spot where she had been scratching.

"It's dark, Ida," I said.

"Use the flashlight, silly."

I directed the beam onto her pussy, and a flood of remembrances washed over me. Ida's pussy, as they all were, was unique. But her's was special. The left lip was noticeably larger than the right. We used to talk about it. We wondered if it was because she was left-handed. Back when we still lived together, I used to revel in licking and sucking the large side, then switching to the small side, then back again. Those were some of the better times we had together.

"Do you see a pimple?" she asked again.

There was an ingrown hair next to the small lip.

"Yes," I answered, "there is a small pimple there."

I sat back and closed my eyes, trying to ignore her smell.

"Well, don't just leave it there," she demanded. "Squeeze it."

Apparently, I hesitated too long.

"I am your wife," she said. "You can touch my pussy."

Before I could contain myself, I blurted out, "That is exactly what I am trying *not* to do."

The disappointment in her voice caught my by surprise.

"But why?" she asked. "I'm trying to give you pussy, and you're resisting?!"

I couldn't think of a way to sanitize it, so I simply said it.

"It's because you might still be crazy."

"You're a fucking psychophobe?"

"Is that a word?"

"It is now," she asserted. "What happened to the man who used to claim that he would fuck anyone even if she was deaf, dumb, blind, cripple and crazy?"

I had to admit, that did sound like something I might have said as a young man, but I couldn't imagine saying that to my wife. She must have overheard me saying that to one of my buddies. And even then, I was blowing smoke.

"I don't know that you're not dangerous," I said at last. "How long were you in that place?"

"Years," she admitted. "I was inside for years. But that doesn't mean I was crazy."

"Well, what *does* it mean?" I asked.

She crawled back onto her mat on her side of the van. The flashlight shifted, and cast eery shadows on the white van walls. The images were broken up at regular intervals by the van's support beams. Ida crawled into her sleeping bag, and pulled the flap up around her neck.

"What does it mean?" I asked again.

Just about the time I figured she wasn't going to answer me, she said, "I was a political prisoner."

"A political prisoner?" I wanted to laugh. "Since when do we put people in the crazy house for political reasons?"

"Since forever," she said. "We taught the Russians."

Now I was curious. What could she possibly know that would get her committed? That was number one. Number two was, how did she get out?

So I asked, "What could you possibly know that would keep you committed in a mental institution?"

I could tell that the question made her uncomfortable. She was literally twisting in her sleeping bag. All at once, she sat straight up and scooted back, allowing the top edge of her sleeping bag to drape down to her waist, revealing her full breasts. I tried to look away, but I couldn't.

"Okay," she said, "I'll tell you."

I was taken aback. I had not expected that there was really an answer. But with what I construed as a defiant expression on her face– I could scarcely see her eyes flitting from one point on the van floor to another– she lit into her explanation.

"Initially," she said, her voice reminding me of the old Ida, the one that had convinced me years earlier to join the Black Legion, "it was the murder I had committed. Killing that honky cop haunted me for a very long time. Years, in fact. But I couldn't tell anybody about it. I had to lie to the folks who questioned me. I had to suffer alone with what I had done, because if I admitted it, I would have to face some prison time. I couldn't come to grips with who and what I was, a cold-blooded killer. That's what drove me crazy for all those years."

Larry Redmond

Then her voice softened.

"Over time," she continued, "I learned to forgive myself and trust that it was okay to be a killer. I read a lot. I studied world religions. I studied different philosophies. I also meditated a lot. Eventually, I studied physics and astronomy. I read Sagan and Hawking and shit by lots of other dudes who thought they were deep, but had no clue what the fuck they were talking about. I was just reading it to be reading it, to fill the days, to help with my self healing."

She stopped abruptly and looked at me. The glow from the flashlight formed small points in her eyes.

"I began researching aliens," she said. She let that statement hang in the air for a long moment as she assessed my reaction to it. Naturally, I said nothing, but her waiting for a reaction made me wonder why. Then she dropped what she thought was a bombshell. "Aliens are real," she said. She used the same tone she had used when revealing that the Adam and Eve story was a cautionary tale, something that, of course, everybody knew. I remembered that she had told me years earlier that she had seen an alien. It was the day she appeared out of nowhere in the vestibule of the house on

Sheridan Road. It was a lot like her reappearance this last time. She still looked good to me after my not having seen her all those years, and she looked good now sitting on her sleeping bag on the other side of the van. That was the day she told me that Nathan Benjamin was the Antichrist. I took her upstairs, and she asked for peppermint tea instead of sassafras, her favorite.

She had apparently forgotten that she had already told me about her sighting, so I pretended to be hearing it for the first time.

"What makes you think that?" I asked.

She played it off. "Don't get caught up on that part," she said. "That's not the part that is important."

"What do you mean not important? That shit by itself is crazy," I said. I wanted to keep her going to see if she changed her story in any way.

"No, it's not," she countered. "That is merely my opinion. And lots of people share that opinion. Having that opinion won't get you committed."

"Okay," I said, "then what will?"

"Proving it," she answered.

Once again, she let the naked statement hang in the air for a long moment.

I broke the moment by asking, "You proved it?"

"No," she answered. "But I did find proof that somebody in the government knows that they are real."

"Proof?" I asked, "What kind of proof?"

This part of the story was new. She didn't mention anything before about the government knowing the truth. She sidestepped my question.

"I've seen them myself," she said.

This part was *not* new. I remembered thinking at the time that Ida was real-live crazy! I wondered if her need to tell this story over and over again was more evidence of her instability.

"I was a shorty," she continued, "maybe 12, 11, 13, somewhere in there. It was around 1955, and I was on the west side. I think I might have been visiting a cousin or something. I don't remember. I do remember that we were on 15th and Drake."

That was right around the corner from where Mo'Dear, Grandma Daughter and I used to live after Daddy died and after we moved from the south side. I tried to remember what I might have been doing that day.

The last time she told me this story, she was outside playing hopscotch with some other kids. As she told it, I began wondering if maybe I should start looking for some place else to sleep. This obsession with the alien encounter could by itself be evidence of craziness. I began to wonder if I could trust sleeping in her space.

"Anyway," she went on, "I noticed a vitamin pill-shaped thing gliding slowly along over the street from north to south. I remember it had Flash Gordon smoke trailing behind it."

I remembered the smoke she was talking about. I also remembered it the first time she told me. All the space ships in the old Flash Gordon movies had smoke that looked like cigarette smoke trailing behind them.

"I pointed it out to one of my buddies," she said, "but she dismissed it as a blimp. Her reasoning was, what else could it be? I knew it wasn't a blimp, but I didn't know what it was, so I kept watching it."

Warming to her telling, Ida began moving her hand slowly through the air to demonstrate how slowly the craft was moving.

"It was moving so slowly through the air that I knew I would have to watch it for a long time," she continued. "I decided that I should go leak, so I could watch it glide to the horizon if necessary. So

I dashed into the house and peed." The hand that was the craft became the hand that was her zigzagging into the house. Then she relaxed. "On my way back outside, I felt a strange sensation, almost like gravity had shifted slightly. When I got outside, the craft had formed a greenish windshield. I noticed it, because before I left to go into the house, the whole thing was greyish-sliver. Now it had a pale, florescent green front."

Although parts of her story at this point were new, the substance was the same. Maybe she simply didn't remember all the details. Ida began looking around the van as if for something of that same color.

Finding nothing, she continued, "So I kept watching. Just then, this creature sat up, and I looked at him." She began moving her head from side to side mimicking the creature. "At first, he didn't see me. But then, he did a double-take, and stared me straight in the eye before ducking down out of sight." She mimicked the creature doing the double-take and ducking down. She sat back up. "He stared at me for so long, I almost waved at him. But then he ducked away. I kept watching hoping he would come back up, but he didn't. After a couple of minutes, the craft took off straight up in the air with no noise, no flare, no nothing. Just zoom! Gone! Like a bat out of hell."

"What did he look like?" I asked. I knew the answer, but I didn't want her to know that I knew.

"He had eyes like a praying mantis, big, dark, and kind of slanted."

"So is that your proof?"

"Not even," she said. "The proof is in the specie of the realm."

"Excuse me?"

"The United States one dollar bill is the proof."

"Meaning?" Now, my interest was truly piqued. She didn't mention anything about dollar bills the last time she told this story.

"If you look very closely at the pupil of Washington's right eye, you'll see that it is composed of the head of an alien being like the one I saw in that craft."

"What?! You have got to be kidding me!" An image of Gilbert Stuart's portrait of Washington flashed into my mind.

"I am not kidding you," she answered. Her voice was calm and even.

"You're telling me that if I get a magnifying glass

and look at Washington's right eye, I will see an alien?"

"Well," she hesitated, "you'll need more than a magnifying glass."

"What will I need?" I asked.

At this point, there was no doubt in my mind what Ida was bonkers. I just needed to be able to show *her* that she was bonkers.

"You'll need a scanner," she answered. "A good one. One that will allow you to scan at least 19200 dpi."

"Then what?" I asked.

"What do you mean, 'then what?'" she asked back. "Scan his eye, blow it up and look at it. It's right there plain as day."

"And that's your proof that aliens exist?"

"No," she answered, a note of irritation in her voice. "It's proof that whoever engraved the plates knows they exist, and that somebody at the Federal Reserve bank approved the design. More than that," she continued, "it means that they might be running the show on this planet. How else could they get their picture on a buck?"

I had no answer to her question. All I knew was that I had to find a scanner so I could look

Washington in the eye.

"That is what *kept* me committed," she said. "I started writing letters to the treasury asking questions, and my options in the joint changed very quickly."

Ida scooted back into her bag, and pulled the flap up around her neck. That was her signal that this conversation was over, so I did the same. I tried to imagine what the front of a one dollar bill looked like. As many one dollar bills as I have seen in my life, I couldn't remember what one looked like in any detail.

"While you're at it," she started up again as if she had been reading my thoughts, "scan the eye of the all-seeing eye on the back of the buck."

"More aliens?" I asked.

"After you look at it, you tell me."

"What should I expect?" I asked.

"Look at the skin around the eye."

"Don't keep me in suspense. Tell me what to look for."

"The skin around the eye is snake skin," she said, still huddled in her sleeping bag on her side of the van. "The eye of the all-seeing eye is not the eye of God, as we have all been led to believe it is. It is the

Larry Redmond

eye of a snake, or rather, a reptilian alien, intelligent creatures from outer space that look like snakes, but who walk upright on two legs like us. *That* is who is looking over everything we do. It is *they* that are the snake in the story of Adam and Eve, a story passed down to us generation after generation after generation for so long, we have forgotten its true meaning. It is *they* who engineered the fall of man."

XI

Wild Bill broke the silence, "You know the story of Humpty Dumpty, right?"

"Yeah," I answered, "who doesn't?"

"But do you know the story *behind* the story?"

"You mean that he was pushed by Little Boy Blue because he was sleeping with Little Miss Muffet and Mary Contrary?"

Wild Bill chuckled. He put one hand over his mouth to hide his teeth.

"Nice try," he said. Then he got serious again, "I mean do you know who or what Humpty Dumpty really was?"

"There's been lots of speculation over the centuries," I answered.

"I understand that," he pressed, "but do you *know*?"

Wild Bill didn't wait for an answer.

"The unspoken sentiment behind these governmental expressions of disbelief in the Johnson shootings," he said, "is that he should have relied on 'the system' to correct what he perceived to be a problem. You see, Humpty Dumpty is the lie that 'the system' can fix shit. *That's* what Humpty

Dumpty is. And it is the king who put Humpty Dumpty on the wall in the first place. The king wants the people to see Humpty Dumpty, and believe the lie, believe that 'the system' fixes all things. The problem the king faces is that the lie is fragile, and it has to be protected. The way you protect the lie is to proclaim that anyone who challenges the lie is crazy. The question that naturally arises is what to do when the people begin to see that 'the system' *is* the problem?" Wild Bill turned his head in my direction again. Then he continued, "We have watched 'the system' fail to adequately address the crimes committed by George Zimmerman, Dante Servin, um, um . . .. Who's that clown that shot Michael Brown in Ferguson?"

"Darren Wilson," I answered.

"Right, right, Darren Wilson. And there was Timothy Loehmann, Daniel Pantaleo, George Hernandez and others to numerous to count. What would lead anyone to believe that Blane Salamoni and Howie Lake II, the officers who killed Anton Sterling on July 5, 2016, or that St. Anthony Police Officer Jeronimo Yanez, the officer who killed Philando Castile on July 6, 2016, would be treated any differently? Micah Xavier Johnson saw what was happening, and acted on it on July 7, 2016. His timing, just days after those recent killings, was perfect. By killing those cops, Micah Johnson demonstrated that 'the system' can't fix this problem, and in so doing, he pushed Humpty Dumpty off the wall. Micah Johnson broke the fragile lie the king is still trying to preserve. Those cops were all the king's horses and all the king's men trying to tape Humpty Dumpty back together."

Wild Bill sat back again nodding slowly.

The timing of our job might not have been as nearly perfect, but so what? Humpty was dead, so we were starting our revolution now.

Wild Bill tilted his head as if he had been listening to my thoughts.

XII

I didn't want to say it out loud, but I simply could not contain myself. I should have told her this the last time she mentioned it.

"You must be out of your fucking mind," I said. "No wonder they put you away! You *are* crazy!"

"You don't believe me," she said. Her voice was calm. She knew I wouldn't believe her, but she told me anyway.

"Aliens are not real," I said.

"Okay," she answered.

"Okay?! Is that your only response? Okay?"

I had expected her to defend herself. I had expected her to fight back. But she didn't. She simply took my abuse.

"Yes," she said, "okay is my only response. You either believe it, or you don't. Most people don't, and therein lies the problem."

"Problem?" I asked. "What problem?"

"Life as we know it on our planet is at risk," she said.

"What the fuck are you talking about?"

"They're here in droves, on the verge of taking us over, and you don't even believe they're real."

"They're not," I insisted. "They don't exist."

"How can you be so certain?" she asked.

The question caught me off guard. I knew the only reason I was certain was a belief that the government would tell us if they were here. But inside, I knew that was a lie.

"And then there was the apple," she said. "What do you suppose that was about?"

The only thing I knew was what the Bible said, and I was *not* going to quote the Bible.

"It was about sex," she answered. "The snakes impregnated earth women. That was the forbidden knowledge. The forbidden knowledge was carnal knowledge, the knowledge that aliens and earthlings could fuck. The apple was a half alien baby. That is what the snake gave Eve."

I didn't know what to say. So, I just sort of laughed. Maybe I had hoped that she would start laughing, too, to confirm that she was joking. But she didn't. Instead, she sat up on her sleeping bag, and turned the flashlight back on.

"The worst part is," she continued, "we're the only ones who can stop it."

"We?" I asked.

"Black people," she answered. "Do you know why

there seems to be a concerted program in place to keep Black people down? A program that has lasted for years, decades, *centuries*?"

Now she had my attention again. This was the very question I had been trying to answer since . . . forever. This was the question Reverend Milton and I had wrestled with. This question is the one that got me working with Menachem. This question was everything.

"I *have* wondered," I answered. I didn't want my answer to seem like acknowledgment of the notion that alien existed, so I tried to clean it up. "But that doesn't mean that I think aliens are behind it."

"Well, they are," she said.

"But why?" I asked. I couldn't bring myself to continue harping on the part about her being crazy.

"Because we have what it takes to defeat them. I believe," she continued, "that they have been here before to take us over, and we kicked their asses. They plan to come back again, and they want us, Black people, out of the way. The battle for earth is ongoing."

I had lots of questions that I wanted to ask, but I was afraid. I felt I was being drawn into a conversation that was premised on concepts I could not subscribe to. I wanted to ask what we had that they feared, but the mere asking of the question presupposed that they existed. So I hedged.

"If they exist," I began, "and have the power of vast amounts of technology, what could we possibly have that would threaten them?"

Her response was instant.

"We are psionic; they are not."

"Psionic?" I asked, "what the fuck is that?"

"Aliens are logic-based entities, like computers," she answered. "We are not. We are intuitive. We are psychic. We know shit without having to learn about it."

"How is that a problem?"

"It is a problem," she answered, "because that makes us unpredictable and uncontrollable. If you cannot predict what your enemy will do, you cannot defeat him."

"Do they view us as the enemy?" I asked.

"Absolutely!"

"But I don't get it," I said. "They have the technology to wipe us out and take the planet. Why don't they just do it?"

"Because they don't merely want the resources of the planet. They want human slaves, and that has been their goal for centuries. They want mankind to be able to work in concert to do their bidding. They want full spectrum dominance."

I was beginning to feel uncomfortable in this conversation. I didn't like the direction it was taking.

"Well," I said, "since they don't exist, the issue is moot."

She totally ignored me.

"Part of their plan to enslave mankind is a program of genetic modifications."

I could feel myself being drawn in again, but I couldn't help myself.

"Genetic modifications on who?"

"On us!"

"Let me guess," I said. "That's what the abductions are about."

"You got it," she answered. "But they have a serious problem."

"To wit?"

"Melanin blocks the instruments they use to engineer our DNA."

"You can *not* be serious," I said. I began thinking again about finding a different place to sleep.

"I am dead serious. It happens that white people

are more vulnerable to their engineering techniques than we are."

"Okay," I said. "And?"

"And the snake aliens use them as a buffer against us," she said. "I'm sure you haven't noticed," she continued, "but white people across the planet seen to have all the power in countries where Black people live."

She was beginning to touch on that topic again.

"I *have* noticed," I answered.

"And how do you suppose that came about?"

I hated that I allowed myself to be so easily manipulated, but I was genuinely curious as to what her answer might be. This, after all, was the very question that had stumped Reverend Milton for years when he was researching the issue. I could hear him again at the Green Mill asking, 'Man, what be wrong with white folks?'

That's when it dawned on me. Ida's answer would be that the forbidden knowledge wasn't simply that aliens and humans *can* fuck. It's that aliens and humans *did* fuck, and that alien genes were what's wrong with white folks. The half alien baby Eve had was the birth of white people, and the beginning of the fall of the rest of us. That's how the aliens

119   Larry Redmond

engineered the fall of man. That would be her answer to the question if I asked it. I decided not to ask it. I decided to merely listen.

"It was the snake aliens," Ida said, "the reptilians. They have been working on destroying us for centuries."

"Can you give me any examples of them working to destroy us?" I asked.

"I just did," she answered, "its on the one dollar bill."

"Aside from that one," I said.

"Their minions," she said, "leave cleverly veiled signs everywhere they go. Why do you suppose Tutankhamun had a snake on his headdress?"

"They were in Egypt?!"

"They *ran* Egypt!" she said. "People on earth are in love with everything Egyptian, but Egypt was the epicenter of the reptilian empire on this planet."

It all fit. As weird as her story was, it all fix together.

"Look at that shit!" she said. "Snakes are everywhere! Look at Tutankhamun's headdress. It is a cobra's hood! It was designed to make *him* look like a reptilian! Look at the symbols at his forehead, a cobra and a snake with a bird's head!"

"Like the sphinx is a lion with a man's head," I said.

"That's different," she said.

"How so?"

Ida was again beginning to warm to her subject. She sat with her legs folded under her, the beam of the flashlight casting stark shadows on her knees, shoulders and chin.

"The sphinx is 5,000 years older than the pyramids, and the pyramids themselves are 5,000 years old," she said. "Originally, the sphinx was a lion with a reptilian alien head on it with a hood like a cobra. It was the symbol of the reptilian empire on earth."

I was enthralled with her story, goofy as it was.

"But the brothers back then kicked their asses, and re-carved the head in the image of themselves," she continued. "That might be the earliest example of the rewriting of history on the planet."

She chuckled at the idea while I recalled the image of the sphinx that I had seen in Grandma Daughter's book years– indeed, decades– ago.

"That's why the proportions are all off," she continued, "why the head seems too small and why the cobra hood on the sphinx has been shortened."

She moved her hands around her head to demonstrate how the cobra hood on the sphinx had been cut short.

"5,000 years after their defeat," she went on, "they came back with a new strategy. They abducted Black folks, and genetically engineered white folks from our genes after discovering that less melanin in the organism made gene splicing easier."

I couldn't help wondering where this tale came from, but I didn't want to ask. I was too wrapped up in the story to want to interrupt it. Ida was psionic. Maybe she just figured it out. I wondered how all of this fit in with aliens fucking humans, and what became of Eve's offspring.

"So," Ida continued, "they flooded the northern climes with newly created white people, and over time manipulated all the cultures on earth so that white people have all the power. It is the goal of the reptilians to have white people act as a buffer between them and Blacks folks. *That* is the game plan."

"Seems to be working," I said.

"No shit?!" she countered.

We both laughed, but she got serious again quickly.

"King Tut was a deformed white boy," she said. "His job was to enslave the people who defeated the reptilians thousands of years ago, and to reestablish the reptilian empire.   He did that.   Skull comparisons have determined that the slaves in Egypt then are the same race of people being persecuted in this country today. Us!"

"And the pyramids?" I asked.   "Are those also symbols of the reptilian empire?"

"I'm not sure," she answered, "but I believe they are the symbols of the alliance between the reptilians and the white ruling class. Remember, not all white people know about this. Only the ruling elite."

"Anyone in particular?" I asked.

"Yes," she answered. "The Masons."

My heart quickened. It felt like *déjà vu*. Ida's answer was exactly like Menachem's had been when I asked him that question in Israel. The Masons! It always comes back to them. Even in the limited light from the flashlight in the van, Ida must have seen my reaction to her answer.

"Are you alright?" she asked.

"I was just surprised by your answer."

"Why?" she asked. "You've known all along that

it was somebody. Why not the Masons?"

I didn't feel I could let on about my connection with Menachem, so I diverted the question.

"Why them?" I asked. "Why the Masons?"

"Because they think like the reptilian aliens think," she answered. "They think the world is geometric and conforms to logic. Their symbol is the compass and the square. That's what that means. Everybody has seen it. Everybody knows it. That symbol, however, is the antithesis of psionics."

"That's pretty obvious," I answered.

"Right, but what isn't so obvious is the relationship of these two schools of thought to the universe."

"What do you mean?" I asked.

"They believe the universe conforms to logic and reason, because at first blush, it appears to."

"And you're saying it doesn't?"

"It doesn't," she answered. "Mathematics and logic and reason do not map the universe, and neither the Masons nor the reptilians can understand that."

"I don't think I'm following."

"It simple," she said. "It is not true that either A or not A. That's one of the prime maxims of formal logic. Either something is true and exists, or it is not true and doesn't exist. But in truth, in this universe, in the real world, it is A *and* not A. Anything that is true is also false."

"What?!"

"You heard me," she said. "If something is true, somewhere in the universe it is also false. In this universe, everything is everything."

"That used to be a saying back in the day," I said.

"I remember," she said, "but it's true."

"And according you, it's also false."

"Now you're catching on."

I suddenly had the strangest remembrance. It was of a young white girl I was fucking way back when I was still living with Ida the first time. Her name was Amelia Walker. Damn, I hadn't thought about her in years! And remembering back, she was also crazy! She was giving me pussy in penance, because a boy she truly loved had left her for not giving him the pussy.

There seemed to be some kind of connection here. When I was living with Ida, I was fucking a crazy girl named Amelia. Now that crazy Ida was trying to get me to fuck her, I was thinking again about Amelia. Maybe that connection was only in my head.

The bigger connection, however, was concerning rational thought. With Amelia, when we first met, she was wrestling with the issue of using rational thought to prove the existence of an I, the individual from whom thoughts sprung. She concluded that it couldn't be done. She concluded that the mind was a Turing machine, and that Turing machines were incapable of determining their own existence. She used Gödel's incompleteness theorem to support her argument. At the time, I didn't fully understand it. Now, here I was decades later, listening to essentially the same argument– the inability of reason to map reality– from the woman I had been living with and cheating on back then, and again not fully understanding.

I needed to change the subject.

"So, how do you know that it's the Masons?" I asked.

"The pyramid is the main clue," Ida answered.

"How so?" I asked.

"I'll explain," she said. "Along with the compass and square, the obelisk is the symbol of the presence and power of the Masons. It is the Masons who erected the Washington Monument."

She was sounding more and more like Menachem

as she went on.

"I know that," I said. There was a tone of mild contempt in my voice, and it surprised me.

"Good," she came back, "but have you ever bothered to look at the top of the Washington Monument? The top of all the obelisks in the world is the shape of a pyramid."

"So what?"

"So, the pyramids in Egypt are the tops of obelisks that theoretically extend down into the earth to Hell."

She paused, waiting for me to grasp the full implication of that observation. I remembered the Caesarea Obelisk in Tel Aviv, made of red granite. It had a rosy color, and I wondered if the red hue signaled some kind of connection to the underworld.

"The obelisk to Hell is the main connection that ties the Masons to the reptilians," she added.

"So, are the Masons Satan worshipers?" I asked.

I remembered Ariella emerging from the far side of that obelisk in Tel Aviv the day we went there sightseeing, and giving me the card that read, *Das Innerste Feuer,* the Inner Fire. Was the *Innerste Feuer* the fire of Hell that burned inside all their followers? I remembered Mighty Red, and I remembered how she twitched when I told her Dietger was dead. Had his death been the death of a little piece of Hades?

"I don't know that," Ida answered. "I just know that the Masons refer to bringing food to the lodge as feeding the goat."

"I've heard that Satan's pet is supposed to be a goat," I said.

"I've heard the same thing," she said, "and it is the brothers at the lodge who eat the food."

"I guess that makes the brothers in the lodge Satan's pets."

I found that notion intriguing, and I think she did, too.

"Anyway," she finished up, "the obelisks under the Egyptian pyramids are the symbolic connection between the Masons, the aliens and Satan."

She paused for a long moment, looking back and forth along the length of the pale, wooden floor of the van. The light from the flashlight spontaneously dimmed slightly indicating that the batteries were beginning to weaken. She looked at me, then looked away. She looked back at me again, her eyes unwavering.

"So," she asked, "are you going to pop this pimple

or what?"

Larry Redmond

XIII

With no preamble, Wild Bill launched into another lesson. This time, his eyes were closed.

"Throughout the history of this hemisphere," he said, "Black people have risen up against the oppression we were all suffering under. Most of these revolts were suppressed, but several were victorious. The very first one was in 1526 in San Miguel de Guadalupe in Florida where African slaves freed themselves from their Spanish overseers. In 1570, it was Gaspar Yanga in Mexico. He attacked Spain's troops until the king of Spain agreed to a treaty. There was the First Maroon War in Jamaica in 1730, and there was the Haitian Revolution in 1791 led by Toussaint Louverture. The last two were ship rebellions, the Amistad in 1839, and the Creole in 1841. All the rest were suppressed. There was the St. John Insurrection led by the Akan people 1733, the Stono Rebellion in 1739, the New York Conspiracy in 1741, Tacky's War in 1760, The Abaco Slave Revolt in 1787, and the Mina Conspiracy in 1791."

Wild Bill ticked off these rebellions on his fingers as he named them, looking down as if he could see each finger as he used it. His hands were dark and ashy, and his fingers were gnarled and bent. I wondered what he did before he got into the pet store business. Picked cotton maybe? Worked as a roughneck on an oil rig? I didn't want to interrupt his story to ask.

"There was the Pointe Coupée Conspiracy in 1795," he continued, "Gabriel Prosser's rebellion of 1800 in Richmond, Virginia, Igbo Landing in 1803, Chatham Manor in 1805, the German Coast Uprising in 1811, and George Baxley in 1815." He ticked off so many rebellions that he had to reuse fingers he had already used. "Then there was Bussa's Rebellion in 1815, Denmark Vesey in Charleston, South Carolina, in 1822, Nat Turner in Southampton County, Virginia, in August of 1831, Samuel Sharpe in the British West Indies in December of 1831." He stopped for a moment, and counted the fingers he had ticked off to make sure he hadn't forgotten anyone. "Finally," he continued, "there was the Slave Revolt in the Cherokee Nation in 1842." He stopped and recounted the ticked off fingers. Satisfied that he had named them all, he went on, "In 1966, the Black Panther Party for Self-Defense was formed by Huey P. Newton and

Larry Redmond

Bobby Seale. Newton himself shot Oakland Police Officer John Frey to death and severely wounded Police Officer Herbert Heanes in 1967. Eventually, most of the Panther leadership was sent to prison. In 2016, it was Micah Xavier Johnson in Dallas, Texas, killing Sgt. Michael Smith, Officer Michael Krol, Officer Patrick Zamarripa, Officer Brent Thompson and Sr. Cpl. Lorne Ahrens.

"Delphene Johnson, Micah's mother, said, 'I love my son with all my heart. I hate what he did.' She shouldn't," Wild Bill said. "He did what he felt he had to do given reality as he perceived it." Wild Bill's tenor voice trailed off, "By most accounts, that would qualify him as a hero right up there with the heros of the past."

I didn't say this out loud, but Micah was certainly a hero to Jiqin and me. Like Twymon Ford Meyers, Ronald Carter and Sekou Odinga of the Black Liberation Army back in the '60s and '70s, Johnson knew what had to be done, and did it. I believed Meyers, Carter and Odinga were the ones who shot Officers Gregory Foster and Rocco Laurie to death on the Lower East Side on Jan. 27, 1972.

Then there was Assata Shakur, accused of killing New Jersey State Trooper Werner Foerster in May of

1973.

I thought the point Wild Bill was making was that these were all true heros of the movement, and I could not have agreed more.

XIV

The following morning, we went through our usual ritual of rolling up the sleeping bags, and finding a secluded sewer to empty our portable toilet. Then we looked for a restaurant for breakfast. Ida suggested that we go to the café at the Lincoln Park zoo.

I liked the idea. There was something about zoos that had a calming effect on me. Maybe it was the laid-back atmosphere, folk meandering from one animal exhibit to another, kids gawking. Certainly, it was not the animals themselves, cooped up in their habitats with no place for them to go, many of them exhibiting symptoms of depression. Maybe it was all in my head. Anyway, that's where we decided to go.

The Lincoln Park zoo had changed a lot since I had been there last. The café was in what used to be the reptile house. We ate a light meal, and it was good. But I couldn't resist wondering where the snakes were. I remembered they had a huge python that was as thick as a man's thigh. Turns out the snakes were on the other side of a small lagoon filled with splashing ducks and a couple of sleepy swans.

This was the new reptile and small animal house. Seemed like an odd pairing for an exhibit.

The sky was overcast, grey and misty. Ducking into the new pavilion felt warm and comforting. The snakes on display, however, were disappointing. No huge pythons, no colorful corals. One or two rattlers and a small, green, tree python. No big deal.

Looking at the green python, though, I began to wonder what reptilian aliens, if they did exist, might look like. I imagined that snake's head being as big as mine. I imagined that snake with a cobra's hood. I imagined its scaly hands and feet, bright green like this little guy.

Just then, it turned its head ever so slightly in my direction. It was probably my imagination running wild, but it looked as if it winked at me. I moved my head closer to the glass to get a better look, but I was too late. It returned its head back to its original position and stopped. I stared at its eye for a solid minute, but it only stared back.

Ida was off looking at a black lizard, and– I suspected– wondering the same thing I had been wondering as I looked at the python. What would an alien modeled on this creature and as big as a man

Larry Redmond

look like?

"That's what they look like," she said. "Just like the Ubaid lizard men."

I didn't know what she was talking about, but I reckoned what I thought she was thinking about was wrong.

"That's exactly what they would look like," she said again.

I felt as if she wanted me to ask the question, so I did.

"Who are these lizard men?" I asked.

"The Ubaid lizard men," she repeated. "They're 7,000 year old figurines of lizard aliens excavated from a site in Iraq. They're about six inches tall, and are clear evidence that lizard aliens ran the show here thousands of years ago."

"And they're still here now?" I asked.

"Yes," she answered, "they're still here now."

"So, how do we stop them?" I asked.

"We do what we're doing," she answered. "Select high-value targets, and take them out. They will likely be Masons, and if we stop the Masons, we stop the lizard aliens."

We headed for the exit. The pond outside the exit was crowded with ducks splashing down, flapping their wings wildly in the water and diving for morsels from the pond bottom. The place wasn't crowded like it would be in the summer, but there were a fair number of people walking to and fro.

There were couples with kids. There were teenagers on what appeared to be a group date, one or two of them with spiked, purple hair. There was an old, mixed couple. He was black; she was white. He was taking pictures; she was tagging along with walking poles to help her keep her balance. There was a man with a close haircut and dark sunglasses reading the plaque in front of the lion house. I stopped short, then pulled Ida with me behind a red and white stripped popcorn stand shuttered for the season.

"What's the matter," she asked.

I nodded my head in the direction of the man in front of the lion house. Her reaction was predictable.

"What the fuck?!" Then she asked, "Is he following us?"

"I don't think so," I answered. "I don't think he has seen us."

"Should *we* follow *him*?" she asked.

The man began to meander in the direction of the

Larry Redmond

old-reptile-house-turned-café. He looked like he was off duty. He wore dirty red running shoes and ratty white jeans. We watched him from behind the popcorn stand. I noticed that his feet seemed long for his height.

"Let's just see what he does," I answered.

He clearly did not know we were watching him. He was too relaxed. After a few minutes, his cell phone rang, and he answered it. His manner suddenly became tense and abrupt. Before the call was even over, he began trotting in the direction of the zoo exit. That's when I noticed that he was pigeon-toed. He ran right in front of the popcorn stand where we were hiding, and dashed towards the street.

As he rounded the sidewalk north, I took off after him. Ida knew to follow. We got to the street just in time to see the rear of his SUV pulling out of a parking space by the conservatory just north of the zoo. We ran to the van, and started it up just in time to see him turn the corner east heading for Lake Shore Drive. By the time we reached that corner, we could see him just under the bridge turning left to go north. I knew where he was headed.

When we got under the bridge and turned left, he was gone completely out of sight. But I knew the way there. I didn't need to follow him. I drove to Mighty Red's nursing home.

We arrived just as an ambulance crew was taking a sheet-covered stretcher out the front door. The SUV we had been following was double-parked in front. The guy from the zoo stopped the men with the stretcher long enough to lift the sheet and look at the corpse. We hadn't stopped yet, merely slowed down, but I could see that it was her. It was Mighty Red. The man stomped his foot in frustration, and dropped the sheet back into place. We drove around his double-parked SUV, and headed west. "Was that her?" Ida asked.

"It was," I answered.

We drove in silence for about a mile.

"So, what's our next move?" she asked.

"You tell me," I said. "You're the one picking the next target."

"We go after the card deck," she said, "the top 52 of the 400 richest families in the country. We'll start with the ace of hearts, the richest man in America, whose creed is, 'All For Ourselves and Nothing For Other People.' The creed by which he lived was the reason he had to die. After him and his entire family, the next seven richest families until we got the whole deck."

"We'll need a crew," I said.

"I'll leave that part to you," she answered.

That part *was* up to me, but I had no idea how to reach my guys. I didn't know where they decided to travel, and they didn't know where I lived. I would have to find all new guys. And since Jiqin had put the last crew together, I had no idea where to begin. I felt lost.

We drove for another few blocks passing grand churches with grey, stone spires, large, brown oak doors, and long, red and yellow and blue stained glass windows, churches I had never seen before and did not recognize. We passed mini-malls where sandwich shops, cell phone stores and bank outlets with cash machines with easy access to money lured customers seeking to shop without having to travel too far. All these little malls looked the same.

My phone beeped. Somebody had sent me a text. It was from Unknown and read merely, "You're welcome." A message like that could only come from one person. Jiqin was back in town.

I keyed and sent, "thx." After a few minutes, I

keyed and sent "where's the crew?"

She sent back, "We need to talk. Let's meet."

As part of the planning for our last job, we set up a place to meet and unit of time equal to 45 minutes. The idea was to have a way to communicate in case we needed to set up an emergency meeting. We wanted to be able to send messages to each other as if they were unencrypted without necessarily revealing the entire content of the message. Of course, all our text messages were encrypted, but this extra layer of precaution made us feel better. I sent, "One unit at the spot," meaning let's meet at our prearranged location in 45 minutes. She sent back, "10-4."

The spot we picked was the Metra parking lot at 119th Street in Blue Island. It was the other end of town from where the my apartment was, so it would be harder to link any meeting there to me. At least it made me feel better to think that.

At that time of day, it was only a 35 minute or so drive from Mighty Red's nursing home. Ida and I got there early, but Jiqin was already there in a green SUV waiting. She bade us to sit in her car.

"This is Ida," I said, by way of introduction. "And this is Jiqin."

Jiqin was wearing a long, tan dress with some kind of African motif. It had the heads of lions and zebras and giraffes and elephants mixed in with African masks, long ones with slanted eyes and hash marks across the cheeks. Her lipstick was the same color as her painted nails, a dark chocolate brown. I had never seen her so dressed up.

"We don't have a lot of time," Jiqin said. "I'm leaving the country again tonight."

"Are you in contact with the crew?" I asked. I couldn't take my eyes off her.

"Yes," she answered, "I know how to reach them." Then she asked, "Have you got another job in mind?"

I looked over at Ida. She had seen me staring at Jiqin, and clearly didn't like it. She remained cool.

"I'm thinking we need to start with the Jekyll Island cabal," she said. "The banking dynasty needs to be destroyed."

"What about the 52 richest families?" I asked, referring to the deck of cards she had mentioned earlier.

"That's still the game plan," Ida answered. "The Jekyll Island cabal makes up the aces of the deck. We are going to be killing the richest people in the world."

"The press will scream about national security," Jiqin chimed in.

"Let them," Ida asserted. "The mainstream media have no credibility anyway."

"Do we want to have a social media presence?" I asked.

"Not unless we can make it, if not untraceable, at least unreachable," Ida said.

"I've got contacts in the BRIC countries," Jiqin said. "I'll see what we can set up."

The notion came to me that we needed more than our one small crew. We needed masses of crews.

"Can we use the Guy Fawkes mask?" I asked.

"We can use anything we fucking want," Ida said. "We are the real life Vs for vendetta. We are declaring war on the Deep State, and we are not going to stop until it and all its members are dead, all the Morgans, all the Aldriches, all the Warburgs, all the Vanderlips, all the Davisons, and certainly all the Rothschilds and Rockefellers."

I wondered how she knew those names. Then I wondered if Menachem knew them all. He definitely never mentioned them all to me. I suddenly realized that all the black revolutionaries of the past, Marcus

Garvey, Martin Luther King, Jr., Malcolm X, had all indirectly been stopped by these same families, and we needed to target them first. I remembered a quote I read somewhere, 'If the enemy could only know that Marcus Garvey is but a John the Baptist in the wilderness, that a greater and more dangerous Marcus Garvey is yet to appear, the Garvey with whom you will have to reckon for the injustice of the present generation.' I knew that *I* was that more dangerous Marcus Garvey.

I suddenly felt sorry for these families, the Morgans, the Aldriches, the Warburgs, the Vanderlips, the Davisons, the Rothschilds, the Rockefellers. I suddenly saw them as pathetic.

The only thing they knew how to do was make money. The problem was that making money was a vacuous exercise. And they were more acutely aware of its emptiness than we were. They knew, because their lives were empty. They had no hopes. No dreams. No aspirations. And since a man with no dream is only half a man, they had to manufacture a dream. They had to create from whole cloth meaning for lives that were meaningless. They had the wherewithal to manipulate the flow of human history, so that became their goal, the enterprise that gave their lives meaning. Manipulating other people's lives gave their lives meaning.

For normal people, inherent meaning derives from providing for family, from bettering one's self, from bettering humanity. For abnormal people, people who no longer need to be concerned about providing for family, and who believe that the absence of that concern renders them *ipso facto* better than the rest of us, there can be no inherent meaning to life, their own or anyone else's. As a result, life for them, their own or anyone else's, had no value.

For normal people, the challenge of life imbues strength, builds character. For people for whom life is no challenge, there is no strength, no character. About us, stories are written, songs are sung. About them, there is nothing more than whatever they can manufacture with money. We write stories and songs about each other. They aren't that creative. They don't know how to write or sing. They steal what creative people produce, and sell it back to them. That is all they know how to do. They are pathetic, despicable leaches. They are the albatrosses around humanities neck.

I felt like an angel of mercy. I *was* an angel of

mercy. Not only was I going to free humanity of them and their pernicious control of the planet's resources and the world's economy, I was going to free them from their own pathetic lives. I was going to free them from their lives by taking their lives from them. Were they to live, they would thank me.

"These are the guys," Ida continued, "that the reptilian aliens are using to control humanity."

I looked over at Jiqin. She looked at me and blinked several times. She opened her mouth and took a breath as if to say something, but no words came out. She looked at Ida, then back at me again. I knew what she was thinking. She was thinking that I was an idiot for believing someone who believed in aliens could come up with a viable plan for crushing the hidden hand. I wasn't sure that she wasn't right. I shrugged, then I looked away.

Jiqin sniffed a couple of times, then rubbed her nose back and forth a couple of times with the back knuckle of one finger. She wiped the corners of her mouth with the back of her hand.

"We probably won't need masks," she said. "And we need to get a completely new crew."

"Why?" I asked. "That crew did a good job."

"That job was too dangerous," Jiqin answered.

"We were lucky that none of us got killed."

"But that's the nature of what we do," Ida offered.

"Yes," Jiqin answered, "but I think we can get the job done more efficiently and with a lot less risk."

I asked, "What do you have in mind?"

"Technology," she answered. "The president can use drones to kill, and so can we."

She went on to outline her plan to get techno-geeks to design and build 3-D printer-generated quadcopters, weaponize them with 3-D printer-generated pistols, then equip them with face recognition software that aims them at a given target. We determine where the mark will be at a given time, deploy drones with the mark's face as a target, then sit back here in Chicago and watch.

Ida said, "I like it!"

"After the shooting is over," Jiqin finished, "they self-destruct by igniting the battery, destroying any evidence of where they came from."

"I like it, too," I said. "I like that plan a lot."

"The only problem is going to be finding willing people with the skill-set we need," Ida said.

"That's where being anonymous comes in," Jiqin said.

"Are you an anon?" I asked. I didn't recall that

she had any real interest in computers.

"Not yet," she answered, "but that's part of what I wanted to talk to you about."

"Okay," I said.

I was about to ask what she knew about computers. But before I could, she said, "This is going to be our last meeting."

"Wait, what?"

"This is our last meeting," she repeated. Then she retreated a little by saying, "Well, this is the last one that *I'll* be attending."

"Wait a minute," I said, "what's up with that?"

"I'm going underground," she said. "I'm going to master computers and conduct my raids using the internet. I'm through putting my life on the line. In addition to killing them with drones, we need to attack their life-styles. We need to attack their bank accounts, their stock holdings, everything. We need to disrupt the corporations they own. All of them. And we especially need to destroy the American Legislative Exchange Council, ALEC. We need to crush them into the dust. That is what I have set as my mission, to destroy all the corporations that belong to ALEC, and destroy the families that run those corporations."

"I like it," Ida said. "That complements what we'll be doing."

"But what about us?" I had not expected myself to sound so disappointed, so abandoned.

"The other thing is," she continued as if I hadn't said anything, "somebody needs to attack local billionaires. There is a richest somebody in every state who controls local politics. In some states, there are multiple richest somebodies. They are connected to the big dogs on Wall Street, because they are all connected. They all know each other. They are all in on the plan. We need to shoot them as well. And they won't be as heavily guarded. They might not be guarded at all. I can keep my skills honed by working at that level. We need to squeeze each and every head of this beast like pimples so that their brains run like puss. Maybe I'll even wear a Guy Fawkes mask."

"But what about us?" I asked again.

"What *about* us?" she came back. There was a tone of irritation in her voice.

Then I saw it. She was referring to Ida being here with me. She was in that African dress, because she had wanted me to seduce her. Instead, I showed up with my wife. Ida believing in aliens and that whole can of worms added to her frustration. But before I could come up with a clever reply, Jiqin started the engine indicating that this meeting was over. She figured there was no point in continuing the conversation if I really wasn't on topic anyway.

Ida got the message instantly, and got out of the car. As she headed back to the van, I got out and stood for a moment looking in the driver's side door at Jiqin.

"Be safe," I said. "I'll contact you as soon as I'm resettled."

"We're still good?" she asked.

"Yes," I answered, "we're still good."

XV

"Make no mistake about it, Micah Xavier Johnson was no mad man," Wild Bill said. "And the characterizing of freedom fighters as mad men is not new. In fact, it is standard procedure. Dare I mention John Brown and Nat Turner on that account. Neither of them was insane, but because both acted on their fervently held beliefs, both were called insane in their respective times. Micah Johnson being characterized as 'demented' was no different."

Wild Bill stopped to catch his breath, then continued. "Black men and women have been getting shot and killed by the police in this country for decades. But now that five police officers had been shot by a Black man in Dallas, the reaction was disbelief, shock, awe. Flags nationwide were at half-mast. Obama delivered remarks at an interfaith memorial service and met with victims' families and with local law enforcement officials mourning their own. He had never, however, met with the victims of rampant police murder. His actions and the reaction from the media and the government underscored the notion that Black lives really *don't* matter, not to the powers that be. But that was about to change. Micah Xavier Johnson saw to that."

Wild Bill and I were of a similar mind on that point.

XVI

I had to admit that I was taken aback by the way Jiqin had cut our relationship off so abruptly. At the same time, I knew she was right. A blunt force frontal attack on the Deep State would never work. More than that, such an attack was virtually impossible. We had to do it the way we had originally planned, individual by individual, family by family. And in that exact moment, it hit me. The Masons functioning as the Deep State were using and living by the quaternary of the magi! Know, dare, will and keep silent! That was why it was so hard to fight them!

I could feel myself squirming in my seat as I drove. Ida even noticed it.

"Are you alright?" she asked.

I didn't want to answer. I didn't want the act of talking to dilute the effect of my realization.

"Are you alright?" she asked again.

I nodded quickly and kept driving. I wondered if Grandma Daughter knew what I had just come to realize. I tried to think back on some of the things she had said back then, things that might have indicated that she knew more than she ever let on.

I recalled images of her burning candles and incense, and making a series of strange hand gestures as an ambulance or fire truck would roar by. It was like Catholics crossing themselves, but different. She would put the palm of her right hand to her forehead, then to her heart, then to her navel. She would say that the noise upset her stomach and gave her a headache, but I knew it wasn't true, because the noise never bothered anybody else. In fact, nobody else would even notice the noise if the sirens were at a distance. But Grandma Daughter always heard them and always palmed herself. She later told me she palmed herself to acknowledge God's intervention on Earth. I wasn't sure at the time that I believed that either, but now, knowing what I now knew, I was sure that she knew more.

I couldn't shake from my mind the fact that Grandma Daughter had used the quaternary of the magi to kill my father, but *that* murder was small potatoes when compared with what the Deep State was doing. The Deep State knew what they wanted: the elimination of Black people and the eventual enslavement of mankind, full spectrum dominance. They dared to do it. They ran and profited enormously from the European slave trade back in the day, the way they run and profit from private prisons today. After slavery, they willed our demise by progressively putting into place laws that criminalized everything Black people did, that led to the incarceration of millions of people, mostly Black men, thereby destroying the Black family, and that, little by little, sucked liberties away from all the people.

And they kept silent about it. Keeping silent meant not only not acknowledging it, but actively denying it. It meant setting up and funding philanthropic foundations to divert attention from the fact that their families were ordering the CIA to overthrow governments in South America and Africa so that they could exploit those country's natural resources. That was what the Masons were about! It was the Masons that Kennedy was railing against in his speech about secret societies. He could have and should have mentioned them by name.

It was the keeping silent part that insulated the criminal from the criminal act. Since they always used proxies to carry out their orders, there was never anything that pointed directly back to them. That meant that in our war against the Mason-controlled Deep State, we had to rely on circumstantial evidence that pointed to individuals and their families. And if the evidence led to the killing of a few innocent rich people and families, so be it. Certainly, enough innocent Black people and families had been destroyed in the Masons' quest for world domination. The coming war was magi versus magi, and the people were going to win. We didn't care who the enemy was or where they came from, we were going to kick their asses!

I needed to see the book. I needed to read it cover to cover. I took the I-290 west in the direction of the storage locker where my stuff from the Sheridan Road apartment was stored. I thought that was where I had left it. I tried to imagine what the book could possibly say. Might it say that the Original Order of the Sphinx was responsible for the death on earth of men as we knew them. Was it possible that I could have been wrong all these years about . . . everything? Was there nothing that was as it seemed? The maxim 'Ignorance is Bliss' suddenly took on a whole new meaning. I suddenly wished I didn't know what I now knew.

XVII

I didn't bother to point this out to Wild Bill, but the Micah Johnson shooting was not the only shooting of police officers inspired by the killing of Black men by law enforcement officers. In Bristol, Tennessee, Lakeem Keon Scott was said to have yelled "Police suck! Black Lives Matter!" before shooting several people including a police officer along the Volunteer Parkway on Thursday, July 7, 2016, the same day as the Johnson shootings. On Friday, July 8, 2016, in Valdosta, Georgia, a police officer was shot by a man who placed a 911 call. The officer was shot twice as he exited his car in response to that call. On July 17, 2016, ten days after Micah Johnson's shootings, Gavin Long ambushed and killed Baton Rouge Police Department officers Montrell Jackson and Matthew Gerald, along with Brad Garafola of the East Baton Rouge Sheriff's Office. Long also wounded three other officers before he was himself killed.

Way back when, Ida and I pulled a similar operation on a little police station out on the west side of Chicago in a semi-industrial area where there were no passers-by to witness and few policemen to encounter. We raided it, shot the officers in the front lobby, and set the station ablaze. Like Johnson, that was *my* very first blow for freedom. The only difference was that I survived, and did it again, many times.

XVIII

"Einstein was wrong." Ida was on one of her metaphysical rants. "He postulated that matter could neither be created nor destroyed. As a point of fact, matter is created *and* destroyed all the time. It's just that the process is invisible to us. Well, not completely. We just fail to see it for what it is."

She slowed down a little, and hitched her butt up so she could get her skirt and panties off, preparing for bed.

"Matter creation," she continued, "is a by-product of universal expansion. As the universe expands, it creates dark matter. There is no space for the universe to be expanding into, and it is expanding it all directions at once. Therefore, either it is creating space or space as we know it is getting thinner. Since the gravitational effect dark matter has on visible matter isn't changing, it isn't getting thinner. Hence, the universal expansion is creating new matter as it expands."

She paused for a moment. "And you know what's funny?" she continued, "We think this expansion is happening out there somewhere. But in fact, it's happening right here right now. If we had a cube that was not subject to universal expansion, it would appear to be getting smaller right in our hand. Eventually, it would disappear. That means that size is relative, and the speed of light cannot be constant."

Where the fuck did she get this shit!

"Matter destruction happens in black holes," she went on. "Subatomic particles get so tightly squeezed by the gravitational force in black holes that they no longer traverse space and no longer spin. They simply cease to exist. Or maybe they simply become imperceptible by any means to us, because they have reverted back to their original absolute size. Either way, as far as we are concerned, those particles are no longer there."

She stopped for a moment, then asked, "Are you listening?"

"I'm listening," I said. "I thought you told me once that black holes are where light got converted into dark matter."

"That's right!" she said. She stopped folding her clothes so she could focus on this new concept. It's as if these notions were coming to her out of the blue. "Light gets consumed in black holes! Light is the fuel! Light consumption releases the dark energy that drives universal expansion, and the residue is dark matter!"

I didn't want to tell her that I thought her ideas were crazy. I sat up straight, and pretended to pay closer attention. I didn't want to explain that I was shifting my attention to the oppressor class using the quaternary of the magi. It seemed to work. Ida dove back into her diatribe.

"Wow!" she said, "that's it! We've just figured it out!"

I tuned out, but I kept my gaze fixed on the bridge of her nose. It didn't work.

"You're not listening, are you?" she asked.

"Huh?"

"Look," she said, "I'll stop talking. We can go to sleep."

I pulled the book from under the blanket where I had stashed it. I felt like a ten-year-old caught stealing cookies. I placed the book on the floor of the van between her pallet and mine. My placing it there that way– my presenting it to Ida that way– reminded me of how I had thought Grandma Daughter must have presented it to me. I was giving her– as Grandma Daughter had given me– the wisdom of the ages, literally. There was stuff in this book that it would take her years to realize the full value of, if she ever did. There was stuff in this book that I *still* didn't fully understand. That's why I needed to reread it. I wondered what could have been on Grandma Daughter's mind as she gave this book to me. I was a teenager. It must have been a massive act of faith for her to give such an important gift to me. I wondered why she hadn't given it to her daughter, my mother. Had she seen something in me that she hadn't seen in her. I was a child! There couldn't have been anything to see! Had the stars been aligned in some special way?

"What's this?" Ida asked.

"A book," I said.

"I can see that part," she quipped.

I didn't know what to answer. How do you tell someone that this book had the answers to all questions, asked and unasked.

"I need for you to read this after I get through with it," I said.

"What is it?" she asked, picking it up and flipping through it.

"It's sort of like a Bible," I answered.

She stopped flipping somewhere in the middle, and started reading. She read about five pages.

"I think I've read this book," she said.

"That's not possible," I answered. "That's the only copy."

She flipped to the very last page, and began reading. After a few lines, she said, "I *have* read this book." She returned her gaze back to the top of the last page, and began reading aloud. "The magi is neither good nor evil. The magi is simply the magi, master of his own destiny. The magi determines what he wants, determines how to get it, then acts on his determination. The magi never reveals his purpose. He, in fact, actively diverts attention from his purpose, especially if his purpose would engender opposition. With careful planning, the magi can be the master of mankind." Ida paused for a long moment, then said, "Yes, I have read this *very* book." She paused again. "Aba gave it to me to read years ago."

A flood of emotions washed over me. I remembered Menachem telling me that Aba had been an assassin for the CIA. He even suggested that Aba might have poisoned my mother. That would certainly explain how he got the book, and how Ida got to read it.

"So what did you think?" I asked.

"It was alright."

"Alright?!" I couldn't believe what I was hearing. "This book was only alright to you?"

"There's gaps in it," she said.

"Like what?!" I could feel myself becoming indignant.

"Like what I was just explaining to you."

"You think dark matter and subatomic particles mean something?!"

"Yes," she answered, "they mean everything."

"Sometimes, I think there is something wrong with you."

"There is," she said, "I'm crazy. But that doesn't change the facts. Life in the universe as we know it is one big cosmic game of hide the ball. We keep looking for answers in the things we see around us, but the answers are never there."

"Then why do we keep looking?" I thought I was being sarcastic.

"That, sir," she said, "is the $64,000.00 question."

Enough was enough. She didn't have the answers I wanted, and I wasn't sure answers even existed. I pulled the flap of my sleeping bag up over my shoulders, and went to sleep.

XIX

Wild Bill pointed out that officials at all levels of government– the president, governors, mayors– were all calling for peace and love. All were declaring that violence won't stop violence. The problem was that all of these calls for restraint were being directed at the Black community. In other words, they wanted us to remain docile while their minions were killing us in the streets. What they meant by stop the violence was stop the violence against the police. If they truly wanted to stop the violence, they would be directing their comments *to* the police, not to us. It was they, after all, who were the primary purveyors of violence in this country. Martin knew that. That's why they killed him. But they won't stop, and neither will we. Micah Xavier Johnson was one of us, a true freedom fighter. We will continue his fight forever.

Crazy is as crazy does!

Just then, Wild Bill blurted out, "Now I see it. You're Betty's grandbaby."

"What?!" I asked. "You knew Grandma Daughter?"

Betty Adams was Grandma Daughter's slave name.

"Damn," he said, "this is my stop."

I looked around trying to figure out how he knew where we were. I didn't even know where we were, and I could see. He stood up abruptly, flicked out his cane, and tapped his way to the train exit.

"Betty Adams was my sister-in-law. She was married to my big brother," he said as the doors closed behind him.

"Wait!" I shouted, "We need to talk!"

That was it! That was why he looked familiar. He was related to Paw-paw, Grandma Daughter's husband. It was his resemblance to Paw-paw that I was seeing, the exaggerated, ramrod straight posture as he walked, his shoulders swaying to and fro. But how could that be? How could Wild Bill know Grandma Daughter? He would have to be a hundred years old, because that's how old she would have been by now!

I leaped up from my seat. I snatched down on the emergency exit handle, and pushed the car doors open. The train was already moving, but not very fast, so I jumped and twisted my ankle as I landed and lost my balance and sprawled onto the wooden platform, face first. I struggled up and, hopping on my good leg, tried to catch Wild Bill.

He was moving really fast for an old blind man. By the time I managed to get to the turnstile, he was already half way down the stairs. I pushed through the turnstile, but by the time I got down the stairs to ground level, he was already gone. It was as if he had simply disappeared.

I never saw him again after that.

Larry Redmond

XX

Ida and I spent the next few– I don't know– days, weeks driving around town living like tourists. We went to movies. We went to museums. We went to ball games. We parked in different neighborhoods each night when we slept. We needed some kind of plan, but conjuring up the energy to make one seemed like too much work. Besides, there was no urgency. We had just pulled a big job, and I needed to rest.

Somewhere along the way, we got burner phones. We needed to be able to communicate with each other in the event we got separated. I wanted to get something simple, but Ida insisted that we get phones with a lot of features. So we did. And it turned out to be a good idea. Sometimes, during the early evening after a full day of playing tourists, we used the phones to see what was going on around the world. I routinely checked news feeds for any indication of the impact our raid might have had on the capitalist hierarchy. I was not surprised to find nothing night after night.

That's how Ida stumbled upon it. It was on Youtube. She had been watching the video of the job Jiqin, Brit and I had pulled, the video that had led her to suspect me in the first place. Then she looked at a video in the 'Up next' column. Its title was Pharm Stand II, and it featured a crew of mostly men attacking a pharmaceutical manufacturing plant. It was not clear in what country the plant was located. There must have been 50 raiders in this attack. It appeared that they had some of everything including rocket launchers and AK-47s.

They were clearly pulling a copycat raid, but this raid and this video were well-planned and well-crafted. All the men wore black masks and black tactical gear. They were all well-trained. Their movements were coordinated and well-rehearsed.

About five minutes into the film, one of the raiders ran across the lane between two steel grey storage vats. He was carrying a banner like one would expect to see in a wild west movie. Only, it wasn't the U.S. flag. It was the standard of the Irish Republican Army, the green, white and orange.

I watched this particular raider for several minutes, because I half expected him to get shot. It looked as if his goal was different from that of the raiders as a whole. His movements appeared to be at odds with theirs. Their movements were coordinated as they worked their way towards some common goal or target which was somewhere off-camera. His movements were generally in a different direction perpendicular to theirs.

The other reason I watched him was that I wanted to know what he planned to do with that flag. It wasn't like he was taking Iwo Jima. It wasn't like he could plant it at the top of a hill after they had taken it.

After a few steps darting in one direction, he abruptly changed directions. He pivoted sharply to his left, and exposed the other side of his flag. The other side was the Confederate battle flag in red, white and blue. The contrast in colors was jarring.

Just then, the video got interrupted when someone jostled the camera. There was a swirling blue sky with structures of some sort swishing by, then it cut to black.

Almost instantly, it cut to some point later in the battle. The point of view was different. Now the camera was pointed at one of the buildings where I suspected offices were housed. On top of that building, the standard bearer I had been watching lowered the company's flag. The flag itself was blurred out, so I still couldn't tell what the company was. Then the bearer raised the green, white and orange with the Confederate red, white and blue on the other side. In the background, thick clouds of heavy, grey smoke bellowed, probably from an explosion set off by the other raiders. Then the standard bearer ducked down, and ran to the staircase heading out. That's when the video ended.

"It's catching on," Ida said. "It already has millions of views. Folks are getting the hint."

"I kind of thought they might," I said. I tried to sound nonchalant, but inside, I had trouble containing myself. I wanted to jump up and down and cheer.

It wasn't clear when this raid was executed, but that evening on Fox News, there was a short mention in one of the crawlers rolling below one of the talking heads that referenced a pharmaceutical plant having been burned down somewhere in Europe. That crawler feed could have been referring to something else, but I suspected not. There was no mention of it being a copycat incident.

The next morning, we ate breakfast at a little diner over on 75th and Exchange. I had eggs and grits and toast and cranberry juice and coffee. Ida had pancakes with strawberries and maple syrup.

From there, we drove over to the 35th Street lake front, and spent the day lolling in the grass and staring out over the water.

Not two days later, another video showed up in the 'Up next' column. It already had several thousand views. In this one, the setting was somewhere out west, Colorado maybe. Or maybe it was a desert in South America. There was no way to know for sure.

The scene looked like a movie of the Little Big Horn, only with present-day equipment. The video began with one of those huge tan military trucks the government is giving away to local U.S. law enforcement racing down a dirt road along an oil pipeline. The truck was being chased by a band of several dozen indigenous Americans in pickup trucks. Way behind the main column, warriors in full battle regalia including paint and eagles' feathers rode on flatbed trucks. A few of them wore red bandanas over their faces. There was an enormous cloud of dust in the wake of so many vehicles, so the flatbed truck warriors lagged back to allow some of the dust to settle before they drove into it.

After a few seconds, the military truck came to a

bend in the road. It was clear that it was going too fast, the big tires sliding in the sand on the hard-packed dirt. One of the wheels dipped into a rut, and the truck began to sway from side to side. Just then, the driver lost control, and the truck flipped onto its side, rolled over, and came to rest on its opposite side. The pickup trucks stopped several hundred feet back, and allowed the flatbed truck warriors to take the lead. These warriors circled the military truck, its big wheels with thick, black tires still spinning, the dust surrounding the big truck beginning to settle. The warriors threw Molotov cocktails on the truck until the whole truck was engulfed in flames. There was no sound to this video, but the drivers from the pickup trucks were out and also dancing around the blaze and chanting. They, too, wore feathers and paint, and celebrated in their victory.

"These motherfuckers are serious," Ida said as the video ended.

My only response was, "I know, right?"

I tuned into Fox News to see if there was any coverage. There wasn't, not even on the crawler.

I tried using Duckduckgo to search for news about an attack on a truck near an oil pipeline, but nothing came up. Not being able to isolate the actual location didn't help much.

Later that week, Ida and I were heading to the DuSable museum. Winding our way through Washington park along one of its black-top roads, we were forced to stop because of a crowd gathering right behind the armory. The armory was in the north-east quadrant of the park facing the park's eastmost boundary, Cottage Grove Avenue. Some people from some Black Lives Matter-like movement in Chicago had erected a makeshift platform, and were haranguing the people of the community for allowing the food deserts in the Black neighborhoods to continue to exist. A young woman in a red dress held forth into an orange colored megaphone.

"We need to control our own food," she said. "We can no longer allow the big food manufacturers to dictate what we eat."

The crowd that had gathered around her was dense and vocal. People listening to her spilled into the road we were traversing, and forced us to come to a stop. Ida and I both got out of the car to hear what she had to say.

She was a big woman. Her build reminded me of Brit, but she had a heavier butt than Brit. The red dress she wore was loose fitting and long, almost to the floor of the platform where she stood. She had long, grey dread locks that settled on her shoulders like a shawl, then extended down onto her breasts.

"They are poisoning us," she said. "They are poisoning us with wheat that has been sprayed to within an inch of its life with chemicals designed to kill the bugs and increase the yield."

"If it'll kill the bugs," someone in the crowd shouted, "it'll kill us." It was a young brother wearing a black T-shirt with "Unapologetically Black" emblazoned in red letters across the back.

"And that's part of their plan," the young woman in the red dress countered. "They want us to curl up and die."

"And the meats are poison, too," the young brother shouted.

It was clear to me now that he was a plant, and that he and the woman in red were working together to get the crowd worked up.

"We need to stop this shit!" the woman shouted into her bullhorn. "And the action hub of that madness is right there downtown at the Mercantile Exchange."

"They don't want to see us downtown," the young

brother shouted.

"You damn right, they don't," the woman shouted back. "They think we want a piece of the pie. They think we want a seat at the table."

"But they wrong," the brother shouted.

"Hell, yeah, they wrong," she shouted back. "We don't want a seat at the table, we want the *whole* table. Hell," she continued, "we want the kitchen so we can bake our own motherfucking pie!"

The crowd erupted. "What can we do?" someone else in the crowd shouted. This person was an old man with a shaved head wearing a green dashiki.

"We can go downtown, and take the power," the young brother said. "We can shut that mother-fucker down!"

"Well, let's go," the old man said. "Let's shut it down now!"

"Right on!" the young woman said as she stepped off the platform and started walking north. It looked as if it were her intention to walk all the way downtown, and folks followed in behind her, the young brother in the black T-shirt bringing up the rear.

Ida and I got back into the van, and continued on our way to the museum closer to the southern boundary of the park.

"Hell of a speaker," Ida said. "I was tempted to follow her myself."

"I hope she wasn't planning to walk all the way," I said.

"That was my thought exactly," Ida said. "That's why I *didn't* follow them."

We laughed, and it felt like old times. Us laughing together brought to my mind a time long ago when we were both still young and idealistic and believed that the world was fair and that the revolution was right around the corner. It had, after all, been nation time, and Colonel North had not yet flooded the Black community with a virulent strain of crack cocaine the use of which would contribute to the ending of the movement as we knew it. It felt like the old Ida was back.

I flipped on the radio. It was tuned to National Public Radio, and they were doing a story on the Chinese yuan becoming a currency of choice around the world, replacing the U.S. dollar. The story went on to explain how Asian countries held trillions of dollars of U.S. debt. In particular, China held $1.24 trillion; Japan owned $912 billion; Taiwan held $153 billion; and Hong Kong owned $122 billion.

Larry Redmond

Together, they held nearly $2.5 trillion in U.S. debt, or nearly 17.5 per cent of total U.S. debt.

Just then, a couple of talking heads came on to explain something about trade deficits and tariffs and the implications of buying and selling goods globally, everything from grains and medicines to cars and manufacturing equipment. As I listened, I pondered the possibility that these countries could ban together and crash the U.S. economy. I looked over at Ida, and she was smiling broadly. The old Ida *was* back. I turned the radio off as we pulled into the DuSable parking lot. We had to get back into character. We were, after all, still doing the tourist thing.

XXI

Sometimes, we forget who we are. Sometimes, in the hubbub of daily living, we lose sight of that which is obvious, that which is real. Sometimes, we get so wound up in the minutia of breathing and blinking and looking around in the game that we forget that it is, after all, only a game. We forget that reality is a dream and that dreams are reality. We forget that we live in a body. We forget that living in it is like living in a computerized robot, that the computer itself is in the robot's head, and that it makes the robot function and appear to have consciousness. The computer gets information about the robot and the robot's environment from a network of nerves like wires running through it. The computer tells the machine what to do. We forget that it can even feel and express emotion. It expresses emotion so well that we sometimes think it thinks it is us. We rarely have to tell the robot anything. It functions independently of us if we let it. And most of the time, we do, because we have forgotten that we are the ones who are, or should be, in control. The robot talks to people, smiles, eats, cleans itself, makes love, everything. We have

Larry Redmond

forgotten so much, that sometimes, we need to be jolted awake.

News of the uprisings happening around the world was the jolt I needed. I realized that I didn't need to read Grandma Daughter's book on the Original Order of the Sphinx. I realized that I already knew what it said. Not word for word, of course. But that wasn't necessary. I knew the words behind the words. I, after all, was psionic. I knew that the Original Order of the Sphinx was– and the book by that name was about– *Seine Kinder*. This book was written by my Great Uncle Buddy King. That's why Grandma Daughter gave it to me instead of to my mother. Grandma Daughter knew that *I* was the returned Messiah.

Well, not me exactly. Rather, the robot, my earthly representation. The robot and I were not the same. We were separate. I am simply that I am. And I always have been, and I always will be. I am the creature in the robot, riding, looking, waiting. But the robot also has an existence. It, after all, sometimes thinks it is me. It only knows me if I reveal myself to it, and thus far, I never have.

Years ago, when I– or rather, when the robot– was three years old, Grandma Daughter was there. I was sick with a high fever for what seemed like days. She had just come from down south on the City of New Orleans to live with Mo'dear and Daddy and me. Daddy had resented her being there, and he would get drunk and beat her and Mo'dear for no reason other than he felt like doing it. It was between Thanksgiving and Christmas, and I had been having a series of nightmares where people were burying chickens and cats alive. I had begun having these dreams after Grandma Daughter had visited a conjure woman in order to get relief from the beatings Daddy was giving her and Mo'dear. Sister Theresa had been the woman's name.

I'll never forget her. She was a short woman. And she was thin. She looked like a little girl in a grown-up's dress. Even her face looked young. She was very dark. Her eyes were what I remembered most. They were big and sorry-looking like puppies' eyes. I remembered that I had trouble looking into them. Looking into them gave me chills, maybe because I could feel the pain of the people she couldn't help, maybe because I could feel the pain she herself experienced. I looked in them, but then I would have to look away. She, too, had trouble looking into mine, but I never fully understood why,

181   Larry Redmond

until now. She saw something in my eyes that it took years until now for me to understand. She saw something that Grandma Daughter already knew, but decided to keep to herself.

She's the one who gave Grandma Daughter the magic that ended up killing Daddy. It took weeks for the magic to work, and during that time I had a series of terrible dreams. In each of the dreams, Grandma Daughter sat across the room in an old rocking chair rocking and waiting, with the light of candles glowing on her grayish, pale, deadpan face, and the reflection of the flames flickering yellow in her eyes. She was in each of those dreams, and she was in the dream I had when I was sick.

In this dream, I, the real me, wanted to leave my body, the robot, for good. I could see the person that I knew to be me talking to the gatekeeper. I was telling him that I wanted the little boy's body I had been riding in to die. I opened my eyes from the dream, and saw Mo'dear and Daddy staring helplessly down at me. I knew what they feared, but I didn't care. Back in the dream, I was an adult and had left whatever room we were in, and was headed for the 'other side.'

The gatekeeper was an old, black man wearing a

white beard and puffy, white hair, and dressed in white clothes. He nodded his approval for me to go. Then suddenly, Grandma Daughter was there and whispered something in his ear, and whatever it was, it made him change his mind. He summoned me back from the 'other side.'

"But I thought I would never have to go back again," I whined in the dream.

In the dream, he whispered something to me in my ear. As a sick child, I couldn't hear what was being whispered in the dream, but I felt as if I were being tricked. But then, in the dream, I expressed an understanding of the situation, and reluctantly agreed to come back to this side.

"You've got a lot of work to do," the old man said.

I now understood that Grandma Daughter had told him that I as the robot was the Messiah, and that is what he told me. He told me that I was tasked with freeing humanity. That's when I agreed to come back. That was when the little boy's fever broke.

Eventually, he, the robot, grew up to be tall and narrow across the shoulders with a thin neck. His muscles protruded and rolled under his russet brown skin like mice stuffed in a leather pouch. His

Larry Redmond

face was long with shallow cheek bones and lean as if a minimum of flesh and skin had been used to construct it. The hair was short and black and kinky and rough to the touch. His eyes were light brown, and had an asynchronous blink.

Later, much later, that russet brown skin grew to be weathered looking, that short and black and kinky and rough hair grew, what was left of it, grey. The curve of his pointed chin and shallow cheek bones, the full lips and bony, angular nose were the same as they were when they were young, but the lips had parentheses around them now. The close set, light brown eyes were more heavily pigmented, and had bags under them. The widow's peak was gone, pushed away by the swath of shiny skin on the top of his head that defined the horseshoe shape of the hair around the outside of his head. Now, the little boy thought of himself as ugly.

The little boy, now a man, thought he knew me, though that I was a messenger of God, known and yet unknown. He had named me Ophiuchus, the thirteenth sign, the thirteenth day, the thirteenth apostle. But he didn't know me. He *couldn't* know me. The best he could do was intuit my existence, and anthropomorphize some of my characteristics.

That is the best anyone could do.

Thinking back on it, I was wrong. Being God *does* make you invincible. Jesus knew that. He didn't die. He merely gave the illusion of dying. And I knew that I, too, was God, and I also knew that I could and would live forever. Old age, like death, was an illusion, an illusion embraced by the robot. I, on the other hand, was as timeless as the universe.

I was also as unknowable as the universe. The nature of the physical universe was such that there was no certainly. Not in the sense that man wants certainty. Man's search for truth is really a search for certainty. And just as the truth cannot be known, certainty cannot achieved. The notion of certainty is a function of logic. Either something exists, or it does not exist. Either A or not A. Ida was right. The universe cannot be mapped using formal logic. In the real world, it is the case that A *and* not A. That is the true dual nature of existence. For example, the character of light is that of both a wave *and* a particle. There is no certainly as to which it is, because it is both. Formal logic, and hence, all of mathematics and physics, is not adequate to map that dual characteristic. The

Larry Redmond

reason is because the laws of nature do not conform to the rules of logic. Mankind's biggest mistake is in believing that they do.

It is that belief that causes people to constantly look for reasons for life unfolding the way it unfolds, as if life were some kind of cosmic syllogism. Life unfolds the way it does because that is the way it does. There is no logical reason. There is no place for logic in the way life– the universe, or anything else– works. Logic is a perpetual trick God is playing on the world. And most of us try to use the trick to find the Trickster. The problem is, He wants you to look deeper than that. He wants you to look beyond that which appears to be obvious.

For example, everything in existence is composed of light. That means that everything in existence has characteristics that are particle-like and that are wave-like. Our collective perception is that things are solid, that the particle-like characteristic of light predominates. But the wave-like characteristic of the light that makes up everything is ever present. Solid objects are simultaneously non-solid, *i.e.*, wave-like, all the time. The only issue is how to capitalize on any objects alternate characteristic on demand. That is the province of the wizard. The wizard knows how to manipulate alternate physical characteristics at will. That's what makes him a wizard. He recognizes God's trick for what it is, and God rewards him with the truth.

I recalled a story Lillian told me many years ago. She's the one who wanted me to become the new leader of *Seine Kinder* when I was stationed in the military in Germany. She had known my Great Uncle Buddy, the founder of *Seine Kinder* after World War I, and he apparently had told her that he would be returning to lead his children, *Seine Kinder*, to heaven. I apparently looked enough like him that she figured the mantle of leadership was mine.

The story she told was one he had told her. He told her that he was in the middle of a shower of machine gun bullets when he saw a light envelop his body, a clear white light that protected him from the gunfire. All around him, his friends were being shot, but he slipped away unnoticed. It was as if the enemy could not see him. They simply didn't shoot his way. Or if they did, the bullets were unable to penetrate the orb of light. The orb of light was like a space-time warp. As the bullets entered, they became slow-moving spots of light that he simply avoided. As they left, they returned to being bullets.

It was clear to me for the very first time that my Great Uncle Buddy was a true wizard. On the battle field that day, he created the orb of light that surrounded and protected him. He manipulated the alternate physical characteristics of the bullets as they approached him, then manipulated them back as they left, all of this at will and on demand.

His writing the book the Original Order of the Sphinx, and leaving it for me could mean only one thing, that I was to allow the robot to be a wizard as well. This book was Uncle Buddy communicating directly with me, not with the robot. That is why Grandma Daughter gave the book to the robot. The book was never meant for the robot. The book was meant for me. And Grandma Daughter knew that I would eventually get the message, because the robot that I rode around in had the book.

During slavery, folks would often ask a new-born, "Is you the one?" The day the dwarf shot me, or rather, the day he shot the robot, he had asked, "Are you the one?" His name the robot learned just recently was Dietger Scheermann. He had been one of Mighty Red's henchmen back in the day. The robot answered yes just before being shot. The thing is, it was answering yes to the question of whether or not it was the heir apparent to *Seine Kinder.* At that time, neither it nor I knew that the real unasked question was, "Are you also a wizard?" To that question, the robot could have also answered, "Yes," had I known that Uncle Buddy wanted me to express my power through it. And had it known the power it had, or rather, had I decided to express my true powers through it, it would never have been wounded in the first place. It would have simply transformed the character of the bullet, and avoided it, the way Uncle Buddy had done in World War I.

But now it was over. My job was done. The robot knew what it needed to know to do what it needed to do. There would be no full spectrum dominance on earth. Not now, not ever. I could return to merely riding around in it and watching its story unfold and waiting for my cue to exit. I was in no hurry. I had and was all the time in the universe.

About the author

Larry Redmond is a writer, photographer and attorney. He attended the University of Illinois at Chicago, where he majored in Philosophy and minored in English. He later attended the John Marshall Law School, earning a Juris Doctor degree. He formerly worked as a criminal defense attorney representing high-profile death row inmates, several of whom were released pursuant to DNA testing. He now litigates civil rights cases in federal court. He is a member of the National Lawyers Guild.

Larry Redmond is a member of the Perspectivists writers collective, the oldest continuously active writers' workshop in Chicago.

He studied Art and Photography at Chicago State University, and became a member of the Chicago Alliance of African-American Photographers. He is a past member of the Washington Park Camera Club, one of the oldest continuously running camera clubs in Chicago.

He has seven children and three grandchildren. His hobbies include yoga and meditation.

He currently works and lives with his family in Chicago, Illinois.

Visit Penknife Press, the quill that can gut you, on-line at
www.penknifepress.com.